CW00818797
Spinster

Also By Bree

Historical Romance:

Love's Second Chance Series
#1 Forgotten & Remembered - The Duke's Late Wife
#2 Cursed & Cherished - The Duke's Wilful Wife
#3 Despised & Desired - The Marquess' Passionate Wife
#4 Abandoned & Protected - The Marquis' Tenacious Wife
#5 Ruined & Redeemed - The Earl's Fallen Wife
#6 Betrayed & Blessed - The Viscount's Shrewd Wife
#7 Deceived & Honoured - The Baron's Vexing Wife
#8 Sacrificed & Reclaimed – The Soldier's Daring Widow
#9 Condemned & Admired – The Earl's Cunning Wife
#10 Trapped & Liberated – The Privateer's Bold Beloved
#11 Oppressed & Empowered – The Viscount's Capable Wife
#12 Destroyed & Restored – The Baron's Courageous Wife
#13 Tamed & Unleashed – The Highlander's Vivacious Wife (soon)
#14 Banished & Welcomed – The Laird's Reckless Wife (soon)

Ladies of Miss Belle's Finishing School
#4 The Spinster (Prequel to the Forbidden Love Novella Series)

A Forbidden Love Novella Series
#1 The Wrong Brother
#2 A Brilliant Rose
#3 The Forgotten Wife
#4 An Unwelcome Proposal
#5 Rules to Be Broken
#6 Hearts to Be Mended
#7 Winning her Hand
#8 Conquering her Heart

Suspenseful Contemporary Romance:

Where There's Love Series
#1 Remember Me

Middle Grade Adventure:

Heroes Next Door Series
#1 Fireflies
#2 Butterflies
#3 Dragonflies

The Spinster

(#4 Ladies of Miss Belle's Finishing School)

by
Bree Wolf

The Spinster

By

Bree Wolf

Cover Art by Victoria Cooper

www.breewolf.com

ISBN: 978-3-96482-056-3

To Friendship
Friends come and go
But true friends are like family

ACKNOWLEDGEMENTS

A great, big thank-you to my dedicated beta readers and proof-readers, Eris Hydras, Michelle Chenoweth, Monique Takens and Kim Bougher, who read the rough draft and help me make it better.

Also a heartfelt thank-you to all my wonderful readers who pick up book after book and follow me on these exciting adventures of love and family. I love your company and savor every word of your amazing reviews! Thank you so much! There are no words!

The Spinster

PROLOGUE

Bath, England 1814 (or a variation thereof)

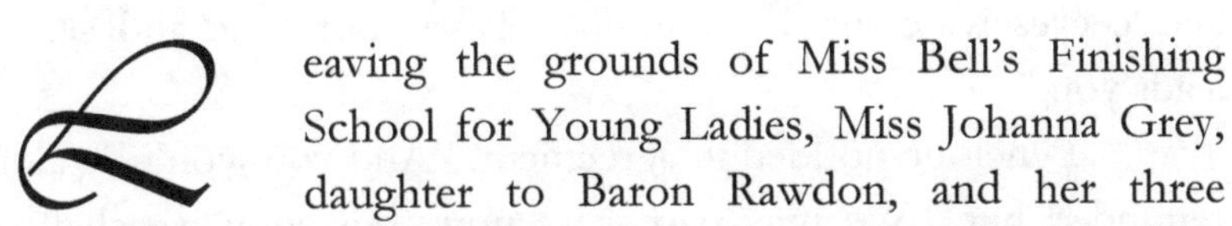

Leaving the grounds of Miss Bell's Finishing School for Young Ladies, Miss Johanna Grey, daughter to Baron Rawdon, and her three friends walked down the street and towards Sydney Gardens. As their last day in Bath was fast approaching, they were all torn between eagerness to begin a new chapter in their lives as well as utter sadness to leave behind those who had become more than friends in the past four years.

"You seem quiet, Jo," Penelope observed, her blue eyes narrowing as her gaze swept over her. "Is something wrong?"

Johanna sighed, "I'm not certain how I feel about returning home. I don't know what…to do. A London season seems less desirable than it did a year ago."

"Oh, it's only nerves," Caroline interjected reasonably, her soft, yet watchful eyes assessing the situation. "It's the unknown."

Jo shrugged. "I'm not sure I even want to get married."

All three girls drew to an abrupt halt, the looks on their faces suggesting that Jo had lost her mind.

"What?" Adelaide exclaimed, brushing a raven-black strand behind her ear.

"Why ever not?" Penelope demanded. "That was the plan. We all agreed, remember?"

Nodding, Jo sighed.

Indeed, they had all agreed to marry for love. At the time, it had seemed like such a life-changing declaration as though they were indeed masters of their own fate. All they had to do was decide what they wanted. Now, however, doubts had begun to creep into Jo's thoughts as she reminded herself that if Owen had lived, she would never have been in any position to choose.

Was she supposed to feel sad that he had died? Was it all right to feel relieved that his death had freed her from a promise her parents had made for her? Could she possibly feel both?

"You don't have to decide now," Caroline counselled, her dark, gentle eyes watching Jo carefully. "Take your time and see where it leads you."

Penelope nodded in agreement. "And you won't be alone," she reminded her. "We may part ways now, but soon we shall see each other again in London."

Adelaide's eyes darkened, and Jo detected a slight quiver in her chin. "I'm sorry, Addy," Jo said, pulling her friend's arm through the crook of hers. "I'm sure you'll be able to come visit us in London." Unlike the other three, Adelaide had no family or fortune to assure her a place among London society. In fact, about a month ago, she had announced that she had accepted a governess position in Yorkshire.

Although they ought to have expected such a development, neither one of them had been happy to hear that Adelaide would not accompany them to London.

"I suppose you're right, Caroline," Jo finally said, unable to explain the feeling of dread that had grown in the pit of her stomach for the past few weeks. With each day that brought her closer to the moment she would once more set foot in Holten Park, Jo had begun to dream of the day that had ended her youth and seen her banished to Miss Bell's Finishing School for Young Ladies.

Four years had passed since then.

But to Jo, it still seemed like only yesterday.

1

RETURNING HOME

undled up in her warmest coat, Jo touched her forehead to the chilled window of the carriage that was to take her home.

Home to Holten Park.

Her family's country estate.

The place of a happy childhood.

As well as the greatest tragedy of Jo's young life.

Snow swirled through the air and lay in heaps and mounds all around her as the carriage fought its way onward. Heaving a deep sigh, Jo glanced at the dim outlines of a world that had once been as familiar to her as the back of her hand. Countless days, her feet had carried her through the tall-stemmed grass in summer and across the iced-over lake in winter. She had climbed trees and found her way through thorny bushes. On rare occasions, she had even dared to swim in the lake, enjoying the cooling water against her heated skin.

Wild, her grandmother had called her, an amused twinkle in the old lady's eyes.

Johanna's mother had preferred the term *unruly*, her straight nose rising in haughty displeasure whenever she'd caught her daughter in a less than lady-like situation.

Still, to this day, Lady Rawdon was not aware of even half of the unsuitable activities Johanna had undertaken whenever she had climbed out of her window and run off to find another adventure. Jo much preferred it this way.

Four years had passed since the day of *the tragedy*.

Four years that Jo had spent away from home and at school where she was to learn *suitable behaviour fit for a young lady* as her mother had phrased it. *The tragedy* had been the final straw, and so Lady Rawdon had sent her fourteen-year-old daughter to Miss Bell's Finishing School for Young Ladies, hoping and praying that for once Johanna would do as she was told.

Four years had passed since then, and Johanna had done her utmost to please her mother and become the accomplished, young woman Lady Rawdon had always wanted her to be. After all, if she had been that young woman from the first, Owen would still be alive today.

Out of the corner of her eye, Jo caught sight of Holten Park, a stately manor with the old charm of an ancient castle. Snow covered its roof and lay draped over the grounds like a blanket. Ice crystals grew at the edges of the many windows allowing in the sparkling light of a sunny winter's day. It was a peaceful sight, always had been, and yet, Jo could not keep a painful knot from forming in her belly.

Glancing across the seat at the rotund and currently-snoring woman Lady Rawdon had sent to escort her daughter from Bath back to Holten Park, Jo smiled, feeling a renewed sense of adventure stir in her blood.

In the past four years, she had barely felt it. Perhaps it was this place that reminded her of the young girl she had once been. The young girl she had buried with Owen.

The young girl that seemed to have survived somewhere deep inside her.

The moment the carriage pulled to a halt outside the snow-covered front steps, Jo pulled her coat tighter around her shoulders and then opened the door before the footman had any chance of approaching. Feeling the cold winter's air touch her cheeks, she breathed in deeply and then hopped to the ground in a very unlady-like fashion, her booted feet sinking into the snow.

Excitement bubbled up in her blood, and a familiar smile claimed her features.

"Miss–"

Spinning around to face Mr. Carter, the coachman, Jo put a finger to her lips, bidding him to remain silent.

All but rolling his eyes, Mr. Carter looked at her, the faint traces of a smile coming to his face as he sighed. His hair had gone grey since she had last seen him, but his blue eyes still twinkled with the same understanding Jo had often seen there before.

After giving him a quick smile, Jo dashed away, rounding the house from the west, her feet carrying her through the deep snow. With each step, her limbs grew heavier and wetness seeped through the skirts. Still, Jo's cheeks shone with eagerness, and she could not remember having felt this alive in the past four years.

Craning her head, Jo looked over her shoulder before she stepped onto the terrace, carefully picking her way across the frozen ground to the double-winged doors. Her heart beat fast in her chest, and old memories stirred, urging her on. Her fingers reached out to touch the silver handle, and she held her breath as her hand closed around it, pushing it downward.

With a silent creak, the door slid open and a welcoming warmth washed over Johanna's chilled skin. Quickly, she cast a look around the empty drawing room, then stepped inside, her heart delighting in the small puddles her feet left behind on the hardwood floor.

Jo knew that her mother would be in fits once she found out that her daughter had sneaked into the house like a common thief instead of entering through the front door and greeting her parents as any good daughter would. Still, in that moment, Jo could not deny the little girl she had kept silent for four long years.

Brushing her boots off on the Persian rug, Jo silently crossed the room and leaned her head against the door. When all remained quiet, she stepped out into the hall and did her best to move stealthily as she listened for sounds of someone approaching.

As though to welcome her home, no one crossed her path and Jo hastened up the stairs to her old bedchamber without a look back. Laughter tickled the back of her throat, and she clamped her lips shut, lest it spill forth and alert someone.

Only when the door was firmly closed behind her did Jo exhale the breath she had been holding, a large smile claiming her face as her eyes swept over the room that still looked as it always had, as though she had never been gone from Holten Park.

Her bed had been freshly made, sheets of lilac and violet warming the room, a stark contrast to the snow-covered treetops visible through the three large windows opening to the east. The wood was a dark mahogany, but thin and elegantly carved, giving the room a feminine touch. Two large shelves were filled with books about distant worlds and adventures that could be had for real if only one had not been born a woman.

To Lady Rawdon's dismay, her daughter much preferred the written word to more lady-like pastimes such as drawing and embroidery. During her stay at Miss Bell's, Jo had made an honest effort to master these qualities so highly regarded not only by her mother but society at large. Still, to this day, her fingers seemed to be possessed by a will of their own whenever she picked up a brush or a needle. Nothing good had ever resulted from these endeavours, and by now, Jo knew that nothing ever would.

"I thought I'd find you here, my dear."

2

A FATEFUL DAY

t the sound of her beloved grandmother's voice, Jo spun around, her gaze wide as it fell on the thin, frail-looking woman who had been Jo's tower of strength all her life. "Grandmamma!" she exclaimed, rushing toward the upholstered armchair where she had spent many rainy days curled up with one of her darling books.

Struggling to her feet, her grandmother stepped toward her, opening her arms. "I admit I half-expected you to climb in through the window."

Surging into her grandmother's embrace, Jo felt familiar arms close around her, holding her tightly. "Oh, how I missed you!" Tears stung her eyes, and she held on to the old woman with an almost desperate need.

"I missed you as well, my dear. Now, let me look at you." Stepping back, her grandmother cupped her wrinkled hands to Jo's face, her pale blue eyes gliding over every dimple, every furrow, every sign that would speak of her granddaughter's state of mind. "You look well," she observed, and yet, the hint of a question clung to her voice.

Johanna cleared her throat and pushed her shoulders back. "I am well, Grandmamma. How are you?" Shrugging out of her coat, Johanna dropped it onto the chair.

"As well as can be expected." Shrugging, the dowager baroness sighed, her watchful eyes never leaving Johanna's face. "Are you happy to be home?"

Inhaling a deep breath, Johanna felt her gaze drawn to the window. "I'm not certain," she whispered as her feet stepped away, carrying her closer to the ice frosted glass.

Outside the window stood the tall ash tree, its branches reaching high up into the sky. Countless times, Jo had used it as a gateway to freedom. Countless times, her mother had threatened to have it chopped down. Countless times, her father had sighed and shaken his head, ignoring his wife's anger as well as his daughter's rebellious acts.

"His family has not been back here since…"

Although her grandmother's voice trailed off, Jo could not help but add, *the tragedy*. Would she ever be able to look at this tree and not see Owen's lifeless body sprawled on the ground below?

Jo doubted it. "Sometimes I wonder what he would have looked like today," she whispered, her eyes distant as she remembered the boy she had known. At sixteen, Owen had been almost a man, and yet, to Jo, he would always and forever remain her childhood friend.

Warm hands settled on her arms as her grandmother came to stand beside her. "He was a wonderful boy, and he would have grown up into a good man."

Johanna nodded, unable to remember a time in her life when Owen had not been by her side.

Their mothers had been close friends since childhood and had found husbands, who coincidentally owned neighbouring estates in the country. Both had given birth to a son within months of one another. However, while Owen had thrived, Johanna's older brother John had always been sickly. He had passed on not one year after his birth.

When Johanna had come along, hope had returned to their small circle, and determined to cling to happiness as well as one another, their mothers had hedged a plan to see their families united always. From the day she had been born, Johanna had been intended to be Owen's bride, and they had grown up with the knowledge that they were to be husband and wife.

As young children, they had merely laughed whenever their mothers had raised the topic. As they grew older, there had been a time when they had openly resisted the union, causing their mothers a lot of heartache. Still, it had been that rebellion that had united Johanna and Owen for good.

"In your letters, you never asked about his family," her grandmother stated, a hint of caution in her voice. "I wasn't certain if I ought to mention them to you."

Glancing down at her grandmother, Jo sighed, "I tried not to think about him." Only too well did she remember the way her heart used to clench painfully whenever her thoughts had strayed to the boy with the easy smile and brilliant blue eyes. Too many days she had spent crying over his loss, reminding herself that nothing would ever bring him back.

"I've tried that, too," her grandmother remarked dryly, "but it was no use."

Swallowing, Jo bowed her head.

"Do you ever think of Colin?" her grandmother asked, her watchful eyes back on Johanna's face. "Or have you banned him from your thoughts as well?"

Again, Johanna's heart clenched, and yet, not in the same way as it did when she thought of Owen. "I tried not to think of either one of them."

"I see," her grandmother mumbled. "I admit I'd hoped you two would write to each other. Shared loss is easier to bear."

Colin Grenville was the only son and heir of Viscount Attington, a man who had all but lost his mind when his wife had died, giving him the son he had always wanted. With his mother gone and his father all but lost to him as well, Colin had come to spend all his time with Owen and his family as their mothers had been distant cousins.

From the very first, it had been the three of them against the world. Together, they had slain dragons, climbed the highest mountains and sought treasures. Always had they stood as one against the often-disapproving looks of their parents. Always had they found joy and laughter in all their endeavours. Always had they walked hand in hand, never leaving one behind.

And so, one afternoon four years ago when Johanna had been locked in her room for *running wild* yet again, her brave knights Sir Owen and Sir Colin had ridden to the rescue, climbing the tower to Lady Johanna's chamber in an attempt to free her from the clutches of the evil queen.

If only Sir Owen had not lost his footing as he had attempted to climb in through her window, they could all have lived happily ever after.

"Perhaps that is true," Jo mumbled, unable to look at her grandmother, "but I think Colin and I would merely remind each other of what happened. I do not think we would be of any comfort to one another."

"Loss should never be faced alone," her grandmother stated, a hint of disapproval hardening her voice.

Turning around, Jo grasped her grandmother's hands. "I was not alone, Grandmamma. I found wonderful friends at school and they helped me see that I cannot live in the past." She swallowed, forcing a smile onto her face. "I must look to the future and move on. I'm certain Colin has come to realise the same. He has his father and Owen's family to..." Frowning, Jo broke off when she saw her grandmother's eyes widen. "What is it?"

Her grandmother sighed, "You know as well as I do that his father is nothing but a shell. He knew not how to grieve his wife then, and he certainly is no help to his son now."

"But Lord and Lady Sawford, Owen's parents, they—"

"They blame him."

Jo's jaw dropped, and she stared at her grandmother with wide eyes. "W-what?" she stammered, feeling all warmth suddenly drain from her, leaving her cold and shivering.

Squeezing her hands, her grandmother nodded sadly. "I know, it is not fair, but everyone has their own way of handling grief."

"But how can they?" Jo demanded, anger mixing with sadness and guilt as she remembered that fateful day four years ago. "Colin did nothing wrong. He was not the reason they climbed that tree. I…I was." Tears welled up in Jo's eyes. "If I hadn't run off with them, Mother would not have been so angry and locked me in my room, and then they wouldn't have…"

"Hush, child," her grandmother cooed, pulling Johanna into her arms. "What happened was no one's fault, do you hear? You couldn't have known what would happen, and neither could they. Owen's parents do not blame Colin because he was at fault, but because," she sighed, "because anger is easier to bear than pain and loss. It's not fair, but it helps them. Perhaps without their anger, they are afraid they'd lose their minds like Colin's father."

Clinging to her grandmother, Jo cried four years' worth of tears as all her bottled-up pain and guilt came rushing forward. Deep down, she knew that it had not been her fault that Owen had died. And yet, her traitorous heart often tortured her, reminding her of her wrongdoings, of her selfishness, of her disregard for others.

Always had she done as she had pleased.

But no more.

If the past four years had taught Jo anything, it was that she was not alone in the world, that what she did mattered to others, influenced their lives as much as her own. No, she could no longer be selfish and ignore the way her acts harmed others. All these years, her mother had asked no more of her than to act according to society's rules. Perhaps it had not been too much to ask after all.

"What happened to Colin?" Jo asked, lifting her head, her grandmother's image blurred through the curtain of tears clouding her eyes. "Did he return home? To his father?"

Her grandmother shook her head. "As far as I know, he left England."

"Left England?" Jo's heart slammed to a halt. "To go where? To do what?"

The touch of a smirk came to her grandmother's face. "To travel. To see the world. Is that not what the three of you talked about for days on end?"

The three of you.

For as long as Jo could remember, people had always referred to them as *the three of them*, and she had been proud to be a part of them. To be one of the three. Today, she was only Johanna. Now, she stood alone, and yet, even on the drive up to the house, a part of her had silently expected to see her two childhood friends rush up to greet her and ask to hear tales of the journey she had undertaken.

"You should write to him," her grandmother urged, her pale blue eyes shining warmly as she looked at her granddaughter. "You're very much alike, and perhaps you can do for each other what no one has been able to do for you."

"Perhaps," Jo mumbled, knowing that she would not write to Colin even though her heart longed to see him. After all, no one, not even her beloved grandmother, knew the whole truth.

All their lives, they had been *the three of them*, a band of heroes, a group of adventurers until around her fourteenth birthday, not long before *the tragedy*, Jo had started to look at Colin differently.

Suddenly, she had noticed the way his dark auburn hair curl in the back of his neck or the way his emerald eyes shone on a warm summer's day. Suddenly, the way he had always smiled at her, bringing out small dimples on the sides of his mouth, had stirred butterflies in her belly. Suddenly, he had not been Colin, *one of the three.*

From one day to another, he had been Colin, a young man like no other she had ever met.

And in rare moments, Jo had thought to see him look at her with the same bewildered surprise she herself felt every time their eyes met.

With that realisation, Jo had once more come to resent her betrothal to Owen. Certainly, he was her friend. Her best friend even. But not the man she wanted to marry. Still, the choice had been taken out of her hands years ago.

And then Owen had died.

3

LONDON AWAITS

Three Weeks Later

"I hope you slept well, my dear," Lady Rawdon said, buttering her roll. "We have a busy day ahead of us." Her hawk-like eyes glided sideways, sweeping over her daughter with pointed perusal. "Now, that you've returned home a fine, young lady, it is imperative that you are seen as one wherever you go. Therefore, I have made an appointment with one of London's most sought-after modistes."

Maintaining a soft smile, Johanna looked at her mother, her back straight and her shoulders back. "Yes, Mother, of course." Out of the corner of her eye, she thought to see a slight frown come to her grandmother's face as though she somehow disapproved of Johanna's answer. Her father in turn did not look up from the paper he was hiding behind. For as long as Johanna could remember, he had been less of a family member and more of a constant fixture in the house–there, but easily overlooked.

Unlike her mother-in-law, Lady Rawdon looked particularly pleased with Johanna's reply. "I must say, my dear, you seem to have become a proper lady after all. I admit I had my doubts when you sneaked into the house upon your return." Heaving an exasperated sigh, she shook her head. "However, now I find myself wanting to compliment your manners. They're a far reach from the wayward behaviour you portrayed before. Your time at school has obviously done you good." A shadow fell over her face, and she inhaled a deep breath. "I should have sent you there sooner," she mumbled more to herself than those seated around the breakfast table with her. "If only I had done so, *that tragedy* could have been prevented."

Inwardly cringing at her mother's words, Jo clenched her hand around the knife she held, willing herself to remain seated, to remain calm, to keep up appearances, to *not* portray the pain and guilt that currently assaulted her heart. Did her mother truly think her at fault for Owen's death?

Don't you? A familiar voice whispered, and for a moment, Jo closed her eyes, taking in a deep breath.

"No one could have seen that coming," the dowager baroness said, her voice determined and her eyes compelling as she looked from her daughter-in-law to her granddaughter. "It was an accident, and no one was at fault there." Her brows rose as she looked at Johanna, imploring her to disregard her mother's words.

"You misunderstood me," Lady Rawdon exclaimed, a touch of justification in her tone as she turned her attention from Johanna to her mother-in-law. "I never intended to suggest that Johanna caused poor Owen's accident. However, the rules for proper conduct exist for a reason, and disregarding them may lead to unexpected and altogether disastrous consequences."

Johanna tensed when she saw her grandmother's gaze harden, silently pleading with the old woman to refrain from a reply. More than anything, Johanna wanted peace in her family and not be the cause for further argument and animosities. Unfortunately, her grandmother did not hear her. "Far be it from me to accuse anyone of anything. However, I cannot fail to notice that your words are contradicting. You say you don't blame her, and then you point out how a lack of social graces affects the outcome of one's life and the lives of others adversely."

Clamping her lips shut, Lady Rawdon struggled to maintain her composure at such an open accusation from her mother-in-law. Her face remained still, and yet, her hand clenched around the teacup's handle in a way that Johanna feared it might break off. "All I said," she finally replied, her voice calm, and yet, there was a slight tremor to it, "was that nothing is without consequence. And while Johanna acted wrongly, she is no more to blame for poor Owen's death than I am." Turning her gaze to her husband–or rather the newspaper barrier he kept between himself and his family whenever possible–she said, "Do you not agree, my lord?"

"Huh?" Lord Rawdon said as he dared glimpse over the rim of his paper, clearly uncomfortable to find all eyes on him. Blinking, he turned to look at his wife. "Certainly, my lady," he replied, his voice growing quieter as he retreated back behind his paper. "Whatever you say."

"There you have it," Lady Rawdon exclaimed, a hint of triumph in her eyes as she turned to look back at her mother-in-law. "Your son understands the concern I have for our daughter." Inhaling a deep breath, she relaxed visibly, the smile returning to her face. "Well, then, with the season beginning," she addressed Johanna, "we need to ensure that you make the best impression possible. You need new gowns for every occasion, bonnets, shoes, scarfs, accessories. We will ensure that you look the proper, young lady you have become, which will no doubt aid us in our search for a suitable husband for you."

Nodding in agreement, Johanna felt a chill run up and down her back. Only too well did she remember the young girl she once had been. In fact, she had felt her echo grow stronger ever since her return home. The moment she had arrived at Holten Park, she had heard her loud and clear and without further thought had obeyed her demands to sneak into the house instead of acting the proper young lady her mother had expected to see. Would she be able to remain that young lady now that the whispers of her past had returned?

Sighing, Jo wondered who she was deep down. Of course, no one remained unchanged over time. Of course, she was no longer the girl she had once been, but neither—Jo began to suspect – was she the young lady her mother wanted her to be. Who was she then?

"Johanna."

Blinking, Jo looked up and found her mother's disapproving eyes on her. "I'm sorry," she mumbled quickly. "I must have…" Words failed her, and she reached for her teacup, relieved to avert her eyes without being too obvious.

"I understand that it is not easy for you to be back home," her mother said, a trace of compassion shining through the harsh insistence with which she spoke. "However, I feel the need to remind you that it is imperative you act according to your station. There is no second chance for a first impression, and many young gentlemen might be put off by a young lady without proper conduct. After all, once married, she will represent her husband's family, and any misconduct on her account will reflect badly on them as well."

Before Jo could reply—not that she had any reply at the ready—an amused chuckle drifting over from the other side of the table drew their attention.

"You seem awfully afraid," the dowager baroness commented with a bit of a mischievously delighted twinkle in her pale blue eyes, "that our dear Johanna will be unable to control any or all childish impulses that might arise. Do you truly believe she would slide down the banister at a ball? Or slurp her tea and chew with her mouth open?"

While Jo could barely hide her amusement at her grandmother's exaggerated predictions, her mother seemed far from amused. "Do not be ridiculous. Of course, I trust her to act with decorum. However, she has acted unreasonably before, and I simply want to ensure that she knows what is at stake."

Meeting Johanna's gaze, her grandmother winked at her before she turned her attention back to her daughter-in-law. "She was a child then if you will remember. Children are allowed to misbehave now and then. It builds character."

"But she is a child no longer," Lady Rawdon pointed out, the expression on her face tensing. "If she has any hope of finding a husband from a good family who possesses amiable qualities, then she will need to portray the kind of woman such a man would choose."

"You mean lie to him?" the dowager baroness asked with stunning frankness.

Jo's eyes widened, and her teeth sank into her lower lip as she stared at her grandmother. Although the argument between the two women in her family upset her, causing her no small amount of unease, Jo could not deny that another part of her loved the way her grandmother voiced her own thoughts with utter honesty and no regard for who disagreed. Was that where Jo's wild side had come from? Had her parents' calm demeanours been unable to conquer the powerful exuberance that her grandmother had passed down to her? Had she been much like Jo in her youth?

Staring at her mother-in-law, Lady Rawdon seemed utterly speechless for the moment.

The dowager baroness chuckled at the sight like a little girl. "Has the cat got your tongue?" she demanded before she leaned back in her chair, her pale eyes suddenly serious as she looked at her daughter-in-law. "I'm certain our Johanna will have no trouble finding a good match, one that makes her happy. I'm pleased to say that she told me that," with a smile on her face, the dowager baroness looked at Johanna, "she and her friends have made a pact to marry for love alone."

"Oh, good heavens!" Lady Rawdon exclaimed, turning accusing eyes on Johanna. "That is a foolish thing to do. Suitability is more important. Trust me, eventually you will come to care for someone who is a good match for you in other ways. You are a grown woman now and must abandon your school girl fantasies." Her eyes narrowed in thought. "Perhaps I ought to have had a closer eye on those with whom you socialised."

While her grandmother shook her head, Jo heaved a deep sigh, realising after years of trying, that no matter what she did, her mother would most likely always find fault in her.

4

THE FAR REACHES OF THE PAST

Venice, Italy
A few weeks later

Standing on the balcony of the apartment he had rented in Venice, Colin Grenville, only son to Viscount Attington, gazed at the streaks of red and orange that hung like brush strokes on a blue canvas. The air held a certain chill, and yet, lately he had begun to feel the promise of spring when stepping out onto his balcony early in the morning.

These early moments were a source of peace and tranquillity for Colin as life kept him busy. Still, he had to admit that he much preferred it that way. With his body and mind occupied, his heart beat steadily in his chest, and the whispers he tended to hear at night were absent.

Art and culture and language and history had led him all over Europe, down well-trodden paths as well as into the *wilderness* where few of his countrymen had ventured before. With open eyes and a hungry mind, Colin had found the world a place of change and wonder. What had baffled him the most was the discovery that right and wrong were concepts that possessed no universal definition. In truth, what one people considered right, decent, appropriate, another would deem wrong, ill-mannered, rude. Often, Colin found himself contemplating the rules of English society, wondering about their origins and whether or not they still served a purpose.

These thoughts often drew him back to his childhood and the two friends who had been more than just friends, but his family instead. Years had passed since those days of childish innocence, and yet, Colin still remembered them as though it had been only a few days since he had last spoken to Owen and Jo.

The day of Owen's death had been the darkest in Colin's young life. Not even the loss of his father had pained him so as it had come a little every day until his father had no longer left his chamber, but spent his days staring out the window. Owen's family had replaced the one Colin had lost, and he had been happy.

Heart-breakingly so.

Their loss had all but crippled him, battering his heart and soul, and he had run as far as he could, unable to remain in England where everything and everyone only served to remind him of what he had lost.

Still, despite the distance he had put between himself and his past, Colin had come to realise that it tended to follow him like a shadow. Sometimes he went days without once thinking of Owen and Jo, but then out of nowhere, his thoughts would be drawn to them, and his heart would ache with their loss.

Owen was lost to him for good. No power on this earth could ever bring him back into Colin's life. But Jo…

Growing up, they had all seen themselves as brothers and sister, and the fact that Owen and Jo were promised to one another had been the source of much amusement and laughter. At age ten, Colin had often teased Owen, who dad scrunched up his face at the thought of marriage.

After all, Jo had been one of them. Not a girl. Not a lady. But one of the three. The thought of marriage between the two had been ludicrous.

Later, it had become unpleasant.

At least to Colin.

Even now, he could not recall at what point he had started to see Jo as more than just one of them. She had always been wild and loud and utterly compelling in her zest for life and adventure, her brown eyes sparkling with mischief as she had led them down another untrodden path.

Still, one day, her smile had touched him in a deeper way, and his eyes tended to linger where before they had not. He remembered well the way his heart had often skipped a beat whenever she stepped closer or her hand brushed his arm in order to direct his attention to one thing or another. He had felt light-headed in her presence, and his breath had more than once caught in his throat.

That change had brought on another as Colin had no longer been able to meet Owen's gaze without a touch of anger surging through his veins. Although it had baffled him then, today Colin knew that he had been jealous, deep down resenting his friend for having claimed the girl whom Colin had come to care for.

Of course, Owen had done no such thing. He had been innocent in all of this. His hands had been tied in the matter as much as Jo's, their union a choice made *for* them.

Colin wondered how he would feel should he ever see Jo again. Would his heart still jump into his throat? Or would he see her as an old friend? Or possibly a stranger he no longer knew?

Of one thing, however, he was certain; that he would not be able to look at her and not feel guilty for in the moment of Owen's death, a small, selfish part of him had rejoiced.

Rejoiced that with Owen out of the way, she was finally free to make a choice of her own. That she was finally free to choose him.

That moment of elation had been immediately followed by a dark sense of betrayal and disgust, momentarily overshadowing the grief Colin had felt deep in his bones. And then Owen's family had blamed him as he had been the oldest of the three. They had blamed him and sent him from their home, cursing his name.

Colin had been devastated in more ways than one, and yet, he had understood. After all, he, too, had blamed himself for the thoughts that had entered his mind, for the relief he had felt even if only for a short second. He had betrayed his friend, rejoiced at his death, and for that he did not deserve to be forgiven.

He did not deserve Jo.

And so, he had left, putting a safe distance between himself and them, ensuring that he would never again be in a position to cause them pain.

And yet, his heart longed to return to England. Some days, he could barely silence it, his limbs restless, unable to keep still as the need for home cursed through his veins. But what would he find there?

A knock sounded on his door, and Colin reluctantly turned from the peaceful scene before him. His heart was still in turmoil as he found a footman standing outside his door, a letter in his hand. "This came for you, my lord."

Thanking the man, Colin closed the door, his eyes finding his father's seal on the back. Still, Colin knew that the letter had not come from his father, but from Mr. Carpenter, his father's steward, who had been overseeing all matters of business ever since Lord Attington had retreated from the world. Occasionally, he would write to Colin, keeping him informed of everything that went on at his father's estate back in England. He would also urge Colin to return and take his rightful place.

Colin had no desire to do so.

Turning the envelope in his hands, Colin noted that it was rather thick, and he wondered what had prompted Mr. Carpenter to fill more sheets of parchment than usual. For a moment, Colin's heart clenched as he contemplated the possibility that his father might have finally passed on. His throat went dry, and a cold shiver ran down his back.

With shaking fingers, he broke the seal and drew out the letter. Unfolding the sheets, Colin paused when he found yet another, smaller envelope enclosed within. This one did not bear Mr. Carpenter's handwriting, but a more delicate, clearly feminine one.

Quickly, Colin scanned Mr. Carpenter's letter, relieved to find it filled with details of the estate and not news of his father's passing from this world. With his heart resuming its normal pace, Colin turned to the other envelope. It did not bear a seal, nor was it addressed to anyone.

Intrigued, Colin tore it open and pulled out a single sheet of parchment. Unfolding it, he allowed his gaze to travel over the lines.

My dearest Colin,

Apologise for my informal address, but my mind fails to picture you any differently than the young boy I once knew. I hope you can forgive an old lady. I assure you it is not meant as disrespect, but proof of the affection I still bear you.

Over the course of the past four years, you've often been on my mind, and I am glad to hear from Mr. Carpenter that you are well. He kindly offered to send this letter along with his own correspondence. For that, I am grateful as I would not have known where to address it.

Now, to get to the reason for this letter, you need to know that my granddaughter, Johanna, has recently returned home from her stay at Miss Bell's Finishing School for Young Ladies.

Colin's heart slammed to a halt, and his fingers tightened on the parchment.

Far be it from me to meddle in the affairs of the young; however, I cannot sit idly by and watch the tragedy of poor Owen's death reach farther than it needs to.

I had hoped that you and Johanna were in correspondence these past years and am saddened to hear that that was not the case.

Therefore, I am writing to you now to inform you that my granddaughter is currently in London for the Season. Her mother hopes to find her a suitable husband before the summer and see her settled.

I thought you might be interested to hear this news. Do with this information as you please, but remember that one tragedy does not erase another and that Owen would have wanted you to be happy.

Yours affectionately,

Grandmamma Clarice (I do hope you remember calling me that!)

Despite the tremors that shook his body, Colin felt a sudden warmth flood his heart. It had been four years since anyone had spoken to him with such affection, and he had all but convinced himself that he would spend the rest of his days alone with no one to care whether he lived or died.

Certainly not his father.

"Grandmamma Clarice," Colin mumbled, belatedly noticing the smile that had claimed his features at the memory of Jo's grandmother, a woman of slender stature, but with a strong mind and steadfast heart.

While their parents had either been disinterested—like most of their fathers—or too intent on urging their children to behave as was expected of them—like their mothers—Grandmamma Clarice had been the one who had sent them out into the world to look for adventures. More than once she had distracted their parents so that they could sneak out of the house. She had read them stories of fearsome dragons and fearless knights and seen no reason why Jo should not also fashion a sword out of a long branch and engage her fellow knights, Sir Owen and Sir Colin, in battle.

All their lives, Grandmamma Clarice had held a protective hand over all of them, her kindness and encouragement granted without hesitation, and they had loved her for it.

Closing his eyes, Colin sank into the upholstered armchair by the balcony doors and allowed his heart to calm. His hands still clung to the letter as though he would be swallowed up by the earth if he dared to let go. And yet, the tender warmth that swept through his being felt utterly wonderful, a gentle reminder of all that he had left behind.

Jo.

At the thought of her, Colin's eyes flew open, once more seeking the words on the parchment he held. According to Grandmamma Clarice, she was in London now, seeking to find a husband. No doubt her mother had something to do with it, Colin surmised, remembering Lady Rawdon's haughty attitude only too well.

And yet, it was the young girl he could still see before his mind's eye who stole the breath from his lungs. Who was she today? Who had she become? Colin wondered, feeling an almost desperate need to once again lay eyes on her. If only to satisfy his curiosity. Could he truly go on for the rest of his life without knowing the woman she had become? Without knowing if the girl he had once cared for still lived somewhere inside her?

I thought you might be interested to hear this news.

Colin's jaw clenched as desire and fear warred within him. What would he find if he returned to England? What if his path were to cross that of Owen's parents? Colin doubted he could be strong enough to bear the look in their eyes. It had crippled him then, and he was certain it would do so again.

And then there was Jo.

She was like a beacon to him, her light shining bright and clear all the way from England, urging him to return to her side. What was he to do?

What did he want to do?

5

FRIENDS REUNITED

fter that painful breakfast a few weeks ago, not another word had been spoken about *the tragedy* or whether or not Johanna ought to love the man she chose to marry. Eagerly accepting the challenge of showing her daughter off in the proper way, Lady Rawdon rarely sat still, her hands always busy as her mind conjured the perfect plan to attract suitable gentlemen.

Although Grandmamma Clarice rolled her eyes every now and then, she refrained from saying another word on the matter, and Jo was grateful for it.

The last thing she needed was a heated argument that would only serve to put her in the middle as her mother and grandmother fought over what was right for her.

After all, Jo herself did not have a clue what that could be.

And so, Jo found that complying with her mother's wishes brought her a strange peace of mind as it saved her from asking herself questions she could not answer. Sometimes it seemed that two minds inhabited her body: the little girl she had once been as well as the young woman her mother wanted her to be. Constantly, Jo felt torn between these two aspects of herself, not knowing what to do or how to act. Frankly, it was by far easier to allow her mother to make all decisions for her and simply go along with them.

Judging from the disapproving look on her grandmother's face, Jo knew that she disagreed. Still, she refrained from saying a single word, and Jo began to wonder if there was a reason for her silence.

Never had her grandmother held back.

Why now?

"It is your decision," she had said upon Jo's enquiry, "not mine since you are the one who will have to live with it." Her pale eyes had held Jo 's for a lingering moment, a message in them that Jo could not quite decipher before her grandmother had turned her attention back to the book in her hands.

Although she tried not to, every once in a while, Jo could not help but wonder what it was *she* wanted. Not her mother or her grandmother. Not society. Not even her friends from school.

But she alone.

Unfortunately, an answer was not forthcoming, and so Johanna soon found herself attending balls and meeting eligible gentlemen, her mother's encouraging nods urging her to be her most charming self. With each day that passed, her introduction to society took on a life of its own, and before long, the graceful smiles and courteous nods became a routine for Johanna, like tying a bow. Something she knew how to do and did without much thought on the matter.

As the music played and lights sparkled in the chandeliers above, one gentleman after another swept her across the dance floor, and while Johanna found herself enjoying the dancing itself, her mind could not focus on the gentleman who guided her steps. One was like another, and the words that spilled from their lips were oddly similar and spoken with the same routine-like politeness Johanna found in her own. Was this what her mother wanted for her? What her life would be like? Polite smiles and shallow compliments?

At one such event—as they all seemed to blur into one another—Johanna rounded a corner to get away from a particularly insistent gentleman and to her utter surprise stumbled upon Caroline and Penelope, two of her dear friends from school. Up until that moment when Jo saw joyous smiles come to her friend's glowing faces, she had all but forgotten their existence.

With each day, Johanna had been back home, her life at school had retreated into the background until it had become nothing but a distant memory, utterly unconnected to her life in the here and now. At school, she had been a different person, hopeful, and yet, practical, making plans with her friends and delighting in their enthusiasm for a happy future. A part of Johanna had believed that she, too, could go to London and meet a man who was her other half.

That she could be happy.

She did not any more.

"Jo, how wonderful to see you!" Penelope beamed, hugging her fiercely. "I've been keeping an eye out for you," she said, glancing at Caroline, "and then I meet you both at the same ball." Shaking her head, she sighed. "Isn't it wonderful?"

Always quieter than the rest of them, Caroline smiled, her dark eyes sweeping over Jo's face as though she could see the turmoil that waged within her friend. "It *is* good to see you," she said in that gentle tone of hers. "You look…well?"

Inhaling a deep breath, Jo greeted them warmly. "I am," she replied, her voice stronger than she could have hoped for as she met Caroline's inquisitive gaze. "And you as well, I hope."

Penelope nodded eagerly, her eyes shimmering with secrets untold. "London is marvellous. Like a fairy tale."

Jo frowned, regarding her friend with curiosity.

Caroline chuckled softly. "She won't say," she answered Jo's silent question. "But it seems rather obvious that she has lost her heart."

"Hush!" Penelope exclaimed. "You'll jinx it."

Jo chuckled, exchanging a meaningful glance with Caroline. "Then I won't say another word. I promise."

The rest of the evening, Jo spent with her friends from school, chatting and laughing as she had not done in a long time. Her heart felt lighter, and for once she did not wonder who she was, but simply lived without restraint, without thought, without fear. Their company brought forth the side of Jo that still had hope and dreams and plans for the future.

Even though she could not say what they were.

What on earth was she to do? All of a sudden, she felt herself pulled into not two, but three directions and no answers in sight.

On the carriage ride home, Johanna let her mother prattle on about what a marvellous night it had been while her own mind dwelt on the decisions she would have to make. For although she had resigned herself to allowing her mother to decide for her, had that in itself not also been a decision?

6

HIDING IN PLAIN SIGHT

till undecided, Jo stayed by her grandmother's side for the better part of the next evening. Dancers twirled around in front of them as they sat off to the side, a perfect view of the ballroom at large. The orchestra played one lively tune after another, and many smiling faces looked flushed with exertion. Still, the atmosphere was almost intoxicating, and a part of Jo wished she could simply join in.

Silently, she had hoped to see her friends again that night, but sadly they were not in attendance.

"You look glum, my dear," her grandmother remarked, her pale eyes narrowing as though she could make out the reason for Jo's subdued spirits simply by looking more closely. "Do you not wish to dance?"

Jo sighed, "I do not know what I want."

The past night she had tossed and turned, her thoughts running wild, burdened by what she did not know. And then sometime in the middle of the night, peace had found her rather unexpectedly as a memory of her childhood had fought its way to the forefront of her mind.

Joy had flooded her heart as she had seen Owen's smile, his blue eyes full of mischief as he had urged her to climb one of the tall trees growing on the border of their families' estates. Eagerly, she had complied, unable to ignore the call of temptation. Even hindered by her skirts, Jo had found her way high up into the tree, taken by the sight before her as her eyes had swept over the horizon where sky met land, always elusive, never to be found.

As she had climbed back down, her foot had stepped on the hem of her gown and she had slipped. For a terrifying moment, she had dangled in mid-air, her feet unable to reach anything sturdy, anything to keep her from falling. And then Colin's voice had reached her ears, wiping away her fear as though it had never been. "Let go, Jo. I'll catch you."

And again, Jo had complied.

It had been a moment of utter trust and certainty. There had not been a single doubt in her mind that Colin would be there, that he would catch her, that he would see her safe.

Jo could barely remember that feeling, and as she woke the uncertainty of life came rushing back to her, making her yearn for the easy days of her childhood when the world had been a safe place and those in it had been by her side no matter what.

Now, she was alone.

Or rather, she felt alone. Could it be that she was the only one who experienced these doubts? Or were others simply more adept at hiding the turmoil that lived in their hearts?

And yet, Jo could not deny that a part of her still thought that the way her own life had turned out was a just consequence for her own selfishness. A part of her believed that she deserved to feel alone.

"I do not believe that's true."

"Hmm?" At the sound of her grandmother's voice, Jo jerked back from her musings, her eyes finding those pale blue ones that were more familiar to her than her own. "I'm sorry. I was lost in thought."

Her grandmother chuckled. "I did notice," she replied, such a youthful twinkle in her eyes that Jo almost groaned with envy. "You seemed caught up in a beautiful memory."

Jo frowned. *Beautiful* would not have been the word she would have chosen.

Her grandmother nodded. "You should have seen your face. Something…or someone made you smile. Who was it?"

Instantly, an image of Colin's smiling face rose before her inner eye, and Jo felt her jaw drop with shock.

Again, her grandmother chuckled, clearly pleased with her astute observations. "And do you care to tell me the name of that young man who's occupying your thoughts?"

Jo swallowed hard. "I…There's…There's no one. You are mistaken."

Her grandmother inhaled a deep breath, then reached out and placed a wrinkled hand on Jo's. "Owen would not wish you to be unhappy for the rest of your life," she whispered, her words like a jolt to Jo's heart. "He was a good boy, cheerful and fair and utterly compassionate. He would be appalled to see you punishing yourself like this."

Jo felt a tremor shake her jaw, and then her grandmother's image blurred as tears rose in her eyes. Quickly, she reached for her handkerchief, afraid others might take note of her emotional state. "I don't know what to do."

"I know, dear." Patting her granddaughter's hand, Grandmamma Clarice sighed, "I can see that you feel lost, and I cannot tell you what to do. But I want you to know that you have a right to live and be happy. It serves no one if you pretend that your life ended the moment Owen's did. It does not bring him back nor does it make anyone else happy. If your roles had been reversed, would you have wanted him to live with this guilt for the rest of his life?"

"No!" Jo exclaimed, remembering the always-present kindness in Owen's blue eyes. "Of course, I wouldn't have wanted that."

"Then don't discount him, either, my dear. He cared for you deeply, and whether you believe it or not, what happened was not your fault. You need to find a way to let this go. It was not within your power to save Owen, and neither was it within your power to take his life. Do you understand?"

Sighing, Jo nodded. Of course, she understood. Of course, she knew that she had not truly been at fault. Even if she could argue that he would not have climbed the tree if she had not run off and then been locked in her chamber. However, according to this line of thinking, one could also say if she had never become Owen's friend, if their mothers had not married men with neighbouring estates, if her grandmother had not always support her in her wild adventures, if…

The list was endless.

Jo knew that the guilt that lived in her heart was irrational, and yet, it was there. Simply because one's mind understood an emotion to be wrong or harmful did not mean that emotion was easily discarded. Of course, Jo wished it gone.

But it would not comply.

What on earth was she to do?

"Why are you sitting here all night?"

Flinching, Jo looked up and found her mother standing before her, hands on her hips and a look of utter disappointment on her face as she glared down at her only daughter. "I…I was keeping Grandmamma company."

Her mother huffed out an annoyed breath. "I'm certain your grandmother would not mind if you danced, my dear. Come along." And without another look back, Lady Rawdon pulled Johanna to her feet and all but pushed her into the arms of a waiting gentleman.

Although displeased with her mother's actions, Jo did her best to enjoy the dance. Although her partner was utterly boring—his only topic of conversation seemed to be his new phaeton—Jo got through the dance with enough grace, judging from the approving look on her mother's face.

However, once the music ended, Jo pleaded a headache and quickly took her leave, weaving her way through a throng of people and away from her mother's watchful eyes. She wanted at least one short moment alone with her thoughts, a moment to take a deep breath, and so she retreated toward the back of the ballroom. There, she spotted a few tall and dense-growing, potted plants, set in a row and thus providing a most convenient retreat for one who wished to disappear…if only for a moment.

Slipping behind the first plant, Jo drew up short when she found that her sanctuary was already occupied. "Oh!"

"I see you've found my hiding place," a young gentleman remarked, an amused twinkle in his brown eyes as he glanced over her shoulder. Then quick as lightning, he reached out a hand and pulled her forward. "Come, before anyone spots you."

Stumbling forward, Jo felt a momentary rush that oddly enough reminded her of her youth, of her adventures. A smile came to her face as she surveyed the young man currently trying to peer through the dense leaves.

His gaze narrowed as he ran a hand through his dark hair. "I don't think anyone saw you," he concluded, his voice low to avoid being overheard. Then he turned and looked at her, a genuine smile coming to his face. "I hope I've not stunned you witless by dragging you in here. I apologise if I've offended you."

Unable not to, Jo smiled. "There's no need. I'm most grateful for this reprieve. My mother can be…a bit trying at times."

Grinning, the young man leaned forward, his brown eyes full of amusement. "If yours is anywhere near as determined at finding you a husband as mine is at finding me a wife, then I assume your assessment of her character is an understatement."

Jo laughed as a strange lightness came to her heart. One she had not felt in many years. "You would assume right, my lord."

He shook his head as though to chastise himself. "Forgive my manners," he said, straightening with a hint of mock formality. "I'm Brendan Pearce."

"Lord Kenwood?"

A frown drew down his brows, and yet, there was a hint of pleasure in the way he looked at her. "You've heard of me? Do I need to be worried?"

"Not at all," Jo assured him, the corners of her mouth straining upward yet again. "It is only that my mother has you on her list of possible suitors. Consider this a warning. If she were to find us here, she'd be most pleased."

"I consider myself warned," he replied with a smile. "And would you share your name as well?"

Jo smiled. "Of course. I'm Johanna Grey. My father is Lord Rawdon."

"It is a pleasure to make your acquaintance, Miss Grey." After inclining his head to her, Lord Kenwood straightened, and his gaze narrowed in thought. "I believe I've met your father before. All he talks about is current events?"

Jo nodded. "Yes, his most meaningful relationship is with the daily newspaper. Sometimes I wonder if he even knows we live in the same house with him." Although a part of Jo wondered how she could share such personal thoughts with a stranger, another part of her felt utterly comfortable in Lord Kenwood's presence.

The zest for life shining in his eyes reminded her of Owen.

Lord Kenwood laughed, then offered her his arm. "What would you say to a refreshment? I promise to have your back should your mother spot us."

Returning his smile, Jo accepted. "And I'll have yours in return," she replied, determined to take her grandmother's advice and live her life free of guilt and regret.

It would not be easy, but perhaps she could take the first step tonight with Lord Kenwood by her side.

In her mind, Jo saw Owen smile at her and chose to believe that he was happy for her.

It was a comforting thought.

7

AN ECHO OF THE PAST

The morning after the ball, Lord Kenwood called on Jo, inviting her on an outing the next afternoon. Delighted, Jo agreed, finding herself quite eager to see the young man again. Still, her mother's excitement seemed to exceed even her own.

"Marvellously done, my dear," Lady Rawdon exclaimed the moment Lord Kenwood had left their home. "He is quite the catch, titled, wealthy and handsome. Many young ladies have tried to catch his attention."

As well as their mothers, Jo added silently.

"Still, so far he seemed quite disinclined to take a wife," her mother continued, completely unaware of her daughter's amusement with the situation at large. "I've never understood why. With his father's passing two years ago, it is his duty to provide an heir to continue his line. I cannot fathom why he would be so reluctant." Sighing, Lady Rawdon shook her head. "Well, whatever the reason, I'm glad that you caught his attention. Now, let's discuss what you should wear tomorrow."

Jo groaned at the consequences of her mother's enthusiasm and was forced to spend the better part of the afternoon trying on dresses, bonnets and shoes. The sun was already setting by the time her mother was finally satisfied and Jo managed to escape her clutches.

"You look exhausted," Grandmamma Clarice commented when Jo sank onto the settee next to her with a loud sigh. "What does your mother have planned now?"

Leaning her head against the backrest, Jo closed her eyes. "I'm certain she's already planning my wedding to Lord Kenwood."

"Ah." Shifting in her seat, Grandmamma Clarice placed a hand on Jo's. "I assume he hasn't proposed yet."

Jo chuckled, "Of course not. I met the man yesterday."

"I know," her grandmother replied, the look in her eyes suggesting that there was more she wished to say.

Jo frowned. "What do you mean?"

"I saw you with him," she whispered, wicked amusement lighting up her eyes. "In your hiding place."

Drawing in a sharp breath, Jo clasped a hand over her mouth.

"Don't worry, my dear. Your mother has no clue," she assured her granddaughter, reassuringly patting her hand. "But I assume you know that if she did, you'd be married within days."

Jo nodded.

"Good. Then the only question that remains is, what are your intentions?"

"I've only just met him. I…"

Again, her grandmother patted her hand. "All I'm saying is that you need to be careful or your decision will be made for you. From what I hear, his mother is almost as resourceful as yours when it comes to pushing her child into the direction of a potential spouse."

"Yes, he said as much," Jo replied with a chuckle. "I'll consider myself warned." That sentence echoed in her head as it had been the same Lord Kenwood had said to her the night before, and a soft smile came to her face.

"You like him," her grandmother observed, her pale eyes slightly narrowed as she watched her granddaughter's reaction.

Jo nodded, seeing no need to lie to her grandmother. "I do. He is sweet and funny and…daring." She sighed, "He…he reminds me of…"

"Owen," Grandmamma Clarice finished for her when Jo's voice broke off.

Sniffling, Jo nodded. "Is that wrong? I do not want to replace him. But last night was the first time that I *enjoyed* remembering him without sadness or guilt."

"No, it's not wrong. It's wonderful. I'm certain he would be proud of you." Squeezing her hand, her grandmother smiled. "As am I."

To her mother's delight, Johanna spent almost every single day of the following fortnight in Lord Kenwood's company. Still, Jo had to admit that it was not only her mother who beamed at the thought that Lord Kenwood would soon cross their threshold once again; Jo, too, found that his presence brightened her days.

With the temperature slowly climbing upward, they often promenaded through Hyde Park in the afternoon, freely sharing their respective mother's delight with their courtship.

"Is this a courtship?" Jo asked one such afternoon as they were strolling past the Serpentine, its waters glistening in the bright sunlight.

Stopping, Lord Kenwood turned to look at her, a hint of mischief curling up his lips. Still, the look in his eyes held no humour, and Jo found herself drawing in a steadying breath. "As shocking as it might seem, I admit that I've come to care for you," Lord Kenwood said, a teasing note in his voice. "Are you shocked? Offended? Appalled?"

Jo heard the mockery in his voice, and yet, the way he seemed to hold his breath as he waited for her answer told her everything she needed to know. "I assure you it is neither one of those, my lord. Perhaps *surprised* is a good word."

Grinning, Lord Kenwood blew out a relieved breath. "*Surprised* I can live with. *Surprised* will not shatter my poor heart."

Laughing, Jo shook her head. "You are quite dramatic, my lord. Sometimes I find myself wondering what it is you truly wish to say."

Nodding, Lord Kenwood drew in a slow breath, his gaze earnest when it returned to hers. "You're right, Miss Grey. I tend to use humour as a way of deflecting unpleasant thoughts."

Holding his gaze, Jo asked, "Am I an unpleasant thought?"

His eyes widened in shock. "Oh, no, not at all. Quite on the contrary." When he saw the slight blush that came to her cheeks, a smile grew on his face that revealed more than words ever could. "Perhaps I can try to speak plainly."

"Do try," Jo said, wondering if she truly wished to encourage him. "And I shall listen."

Inhaling a shuddering breath, Lord Kenwood nodded. "Well, then. To be frank, I've come to care for you, Miss Grey, and by now, it is not only my mother who is hoping for a happy outcome of our courtship. I've enjoyed your company immensely this past fortnight, and I'm hoping you'll grant me the pleasure of your presence for many days to come."

"I've enjoyed your company as well," Jo said honestly, realising that the thought of him absent from her life pained her greatly. As strange as it was, Lord Kenwood had become her sole reason for rising each morning with a smile on her face. Who would she be if he ever left?

"It would be an honour," he whispered, his dark brown eyes holding hers, "if you would call me Brendan."

Smiling, Jo nodded. "But then you must call me Johanna."

"I shall," Brendan beamed, his gaze momentarily shifting over their surroundings, and before Jo knew what was happening, he leaned in and gave her a quick kiss on the mouth. It felt warm and soft and safe. "I hope this was not too untoward." A slight frown rested on his face as he watched her, all but holding his breath.

Jo smiled, pleasantly surprised by her first kiss. "Not at all."

Pulling her hand once more through the crook of his arm, Brendan guided her farther down the path, his gaze often veering to meet hers as Jo contemplated the future that was now offered to her. Would she truly be able to marry for love?

Certainly, there was little doubt in her mind that before long Brendan would ask for her hand. That, he had made quite clear. But what would she say? Did she dare seek out happiness and marry a man she cared for?

Jo knew exactly what her friends from school would say, and a deep smile claimed her face.

Back on English soil, Colin felt as though now *he* was the foreigner setting foot into an unknown land. Although he was all too familiar with English society—thanks to his relentless tutor following his every step—Colin knew very little about what to expect from those he had left behind.

Thanks to Grandmamma Clarice's letter, he could rest assured that there would be at least one welcoming face upon his return to London. Still, Colin could not help but wonder if his father would even recognise him. Would Owen's parents curse his name should their paths cross by happenstance? Although Colin had no intention of seeking them out, he could not help but wonder if fate would throw them in his path, nonetheless. As they had made it quite clear what they thought of him when they had sent him from their home after Owen's death, Colin did not expect politeness in any form. Not that he blamed them.

And then there was Johanna.

Jo.

Ever since receiving her grandmother's letter, Colin had been unable to keep the memories of their shared youth at bay. Every night, he had dreamed of her and Owen, and every morning when he had awakened, he had longed for nothing more but to return to that point in his life when all had been well.

With each mile that he had ventured closer to England, the need to see her had grown. Would he recognise the young girl in the woman she had become? Would their eyes meet, and the old familiarity with one another return? Would she still be able to see into his heart? Or would they meet as strangers?

That thought plagued Colin the most. Ultimately, he could accept the hatred of Owen's parents or his father's indifference as they were already-known facts. They would not take his heart by surprise for it had already suffered for them.

But Jo, she still held sway over him, and he burnt to know how it would feel to lay eyes on her again, to be in the same room with her, to see her smile.

If only the horses could move with greater speed!

8

TURNING OVER A NEW PAGE

Descending the staircase, Jo stopped when she caught sight of Brendan striding across the hall, a tremor shaking his hands. Still, even from up here, she could see the smile that clung to his features as though he had found a pot of gold at the end of a rainbow. "Brendan?" she called quietly so as not to alert her mother.

At the sound of her voice, he stopped in his tracks, his eyes finding hers with efficient accuracy. "Johanna," he exclaimed, hurrying toward her and offering his hand the moment she stepped off the last step.

"I wasn't expecting you so soon." Searching his face, she tried to understand what was going on. "Let me just get my jacket and bonnet."

As she tried to step away, he held her back. "There's no need," he replied, his voice throaty, almost breathless. "If you don't mind, I would like to have a word with you." He swallowed. "In private."

Jo's eyes narrowed. "Why? Is something wrong?"

"Not at all," Brendan assured her, suddenly unable to suppress the grin that stole onto his face. "I've just come from speaking to your father."

"Oh!" was all Johanna could manage as realisation dawned. While her heart seemed to pick up its pace, her mind slowed down, barely able to form a coherent thought. Before she knew it, Jo stood in her parents' drawing room and Brendan took a knee, her right hand clasped in his as he looked up at her with shining eyes.

The words he spoke were beautiful, and yet, Johanna had trouble holding on to them. They slipped away before she could make sense of them. Still, the warmth of his hand on hers felt safe and reassuring. His brown eyes shone with devotion, and Johanna felt herself warm at the thought of having him by her side for all the days to come.

"I cannot imagine spending the rest of my life without you," Brendan told her, his face aglow with happiness as well as a hint of tension, "please do me the honour of accepting my hand."

Seeing the honest regard he had for her in his eyes, Johanna smiled, her other hand settling on his as it held hers. In her mind's eye, she could see the smiling faces of her friends as they cheered her on, remembering how they had each vowed to marry for love. At the time, it had not seemed possible. But now?

This was her chance. If ever Jo could be happy again, it was with this wonderful man right here. All she had to do was say *yes*.

At the thought, her heart skipped a beat, and a warm smile drew up the corners of her mouth. She felt Brendan's hand relax and saw utter joy come to his eyes as he read her answer before she had given it. Inhaling a deep breath, Jo sighed, "That was beautiful, Brendan. Of course, I'll accept."

Rising to his feet, Brendan swept her into his arms and swung her in a circle, his happiness intoxicating, like a drug stealing into her blood and infecting her as well.

Laughter flew from Johanna's lips as she returned his embrace. "Stop! You'll lose your step, and we'll both crash to the ground."

Setting her back down, Brendan gazed down at her, holding both her hands in his. "I know it's a cliché, but you've made me the happiest man alive."

"I'm glad–"

A knock interrupted their joyous moment.

"Excuse me, Miss Grey," Jackson, their butler, apologised with a slight nod, his eyes distant as though he had no clue what had just happened in the drawing room, "but there's a Lord Ashfield here to see you."

Johanna's heart slammed to a halt, and she would have dropped to the ground like a sack of potatoes if Brendan had not been holding on to her hands. "Colin," she whispered under her breath as the world began to spin.

"Are you all right?" Brendan asked, concern coming to his eyes. "Who is he?"

"He…" All but gasping for breath, Jo tried to focus her thoughts. "He's an old friend," she finally said, lifting her gaze to meet Brendan's. "We grew up together, but I haven't seen him in years." She tried to swallow the lump in her throat, but it refused to budge. "I didn't even know he was back in England."

Brendan smiled at her. "Then his appearance here must be quite the shock for you." Turning to look at Jackson, he said, "Would you have some tea and biscuits brought in? I think Miss Grey could use a refreshment."

"Certainly," Jackson replied with a slight bow. "What am I to tell Lord Ashfield?"

Before Jo could will herself to speak, Brendan said, "Send him in." Then he turned to look at her, a smile on his face as he squeezed her hands. "You two can catch up while I go and inform my mother." A wicked gleam came to his eyes. "You do not have your heart set on arranging your own wedding, do you?"

A chuckle left his lips, and Jo did her best to smile while her heart seemed to be faltering in her chest. Was this what a heart attack felt like?

And then the door opened, and from one moment to the next, Colin Grenville, only son to Lord Attington, was suddenly back in Johanna's life.

After four years.

Was this a dream? Was she ill and hallucinating?

Stepping into the room, Colin's emerald gaze found hers with lightning speed. For a short moment, he seemed to pause, drawing in a slow breath, as though their reunion had knocked the air from his lungs as well.

His dark auburn hair lay in fluid waves upon his head, a far cry from the unruly mess Jo remembered. His attire, too, spoke of a young gentleman and not of a boy running wild. Still, Jo could see something of the boy she had once known lurk beneath the surface of this tall stranger. He stood with purpose, his shoulders broad and his chin raised, as his gaze took in the room without ever leaving hers. Clearing his throat, he stepped forward. "I bid you a good day, Jo. It has been a long time."

"Hello," Jo breathed, wondering if he had even heard her, her voice almost inaudible even to her own ears.

A moment of silence followed…and then stretched into another.

Brendan cleared his throat, and Jo blinked.

Forcing her gaze away from Colin, she swallowed, seeing her fiancé's eyes narrow in confusion before they glanced sideways to look at their visitor. Colin in turn seemed only to see her, his gaze on hers whenever she dared look at him.

"Oh, pardon me," Jo said, trying her best to give Brendan a relaxed smile. "Brendan, this is Colin Grenville, Baron Ashfield, an…an old friend."

Colin's gaze narrowed for a split second before it swung sideways, taking in the man beside her for the first time.

"Colin," Jo whispered, wondering how long it had been since she had last spoken his name…in his presence, "this is Brendan Pearce, Viscount Kenwood, my…fiancé."

Looking at Colin only out of the corner of her eye, Jo wondered about the tension that suddenly seemed to grip him. His gaze hardened, and the muscle in his jaw twitched.

"It's a pleasure to make your acquaintance," Brendan chimed in, a polite smile directed at Colin. "I hear you've been on the continent." He glanced at Johanna. "I would love to stay, but I'm afraid my mother is expecting me."

"Give her my best," Jo mumbled, more from habit than actual care as Brendan took his leave, giving her hands a gentle squeeze before he walked out the door.

The moment he was gone, Colin stepped forward, his eyes hard as they held hers. "How long have you been engaged?"

9

NOT IN THE NICK OF TIME

The woman before him was a far cry from the girl Colin remembered.

Although her eyes still shone with the same strength as before, accentuating the dark golden shine of her unruly curls and the soft glow of her sun-warmed skin, she seemed a frightened creature. Her chin no longer rose in defiance, nor did she move with that confidence of someone who was at peace with oneself. Instead, sadness and uncertainty clung to her features, and she barely dared meet his eyes as though she feared his judgement.

And yet, Colin's soul recognised her as though they had been together every day for the past four years. The look in her eyes instantly brought back the memories of their shared youth, and he could see plain as day the pain they still caused her.

Same as him.

The bond was still there, and Colin felt it in every fibre of his body, and then she spoke, shattering his world once again. "Colin, this is Brendan Pearce, Viscount Kenwood, my…fiancé."

Anger gripped him, and he had to fight the urge to grab her and shake her until her teeth chattered. How dare she enter into an engagement when he had been rushing back to London with all haste in order to see her? To…? Did she not know how much she meant to him? Did she not feel the same?

Inhaling a deep breath, Colin felt his muscles tense as his gaze sought hers; however, she refused to look at him and he wondered if she knew how devastating her news was to him.

Dimly, Colin was aware that Kenwood−or whatever his name was? −was speaking. The words, however, never reached Colin's mind. Only when the other man walked out the door did his mind regain control, urging him to remain calm so as to get the answers he sought.

With purpose in his step, Colin moved toward her and her eyes swung around to meet his as though he had slapped her. "How long have you been engaged?"

Her throat worked as she swallowed. Then her lips parted, and three words flew out. "Perhaps ten minutes."

Colin's jaw dropped, and he groaned as though that man Kenwood had punched him in the stomach. "Ten minutes?" he demanded, barely aware of the harshness of his tone as he advanced on her. "Ten minutes?"

Jo's eyes widened as she took a step backwards before her feet suddenly stilled. A small flame sparked in her dark eyes, and her chin rose a fraction as she met his eyes.

Unable not to, Colin rejoiced. This was the woman he remembered!

"Do not snap at me like this, Colin Grenville," she rebuked him, hands rising to settle on her hips, "or I shall have you removed from my home. Is that clear?" A small flame burnt in her eyes, one Colin remembered only too well.

A smile stole onto his face. "I've missed you, Jo," he whispered as he looked down at her, feeling the same flutter in his belly that he had felt before–shortly before Owen's death. "You always had a way with words."

The left corner of her mouth quirked as though she wished to smile, but the look on her face remained hard, cautious perhaps. "Why are you here?" she asked, and her voice seemed to falter just a bit on the last word.

"Do you want me to go?" Colin dared her, remembering the ease with which they used to speak.

Her eyes narrowed, and he knew that she felt it, too. "I did not say that. Do not put words in my mouth."

A chuckle rose from his lips, and as though no time had passed, he reached out and tucked a stray curl behind her ear. "I see you have not changed." It was more of a question than a statement, but he wanted to believe it with all his heart.

The moment his fingers brushed by her ear, Jo sucked in a sharp breath before she dropped her gaze and stepped around him, walking to the window, her back to him. "Why have you come?" she asked once more, and he thought to detect a hint of apprehension in her voice.

Unable to bear the distance between them, Colin went after her. His hand reached for her arm, pulling her back around to face him. "I've come to see *you*. I came the moment I heard you'd returned to London."

Her eyes narrowed. "You heard? From whom?"

"Does it matter?"

"You never even wrote to me, and now you came all this way only to see me?" She shook her head, trying to step back, but his hand held her to him. "You'll excuse me if I have trouble believing this."

Searching her face, Colin tried to understand the source of her anger. "You didn't write to me either if I may remind you."

Her mouth clamped shut as though he had just caught her in a lie. "I didn't know where you were."

His gaze remained locked on hers, their eyes speaking more truthfully than their words. "That's an excuse. You didn't write to me because of Owen."

"Owen?" Her brows knitted together.

Colin swallowed hard. Never before had he spoken about his oldest friend to anyone. "You…you blame me for his death?"

"What?" Her eyes widened in shock, and the air rushed from her lungs that for a moment he feared she would faint. "Why would you think that? I never blamed you. I never once thought…" Tears came to her eyes, and she blinked them rapidly. "I know that Owen's parents blamed you, but they were wrong. You were always a good friend to Owen, and he did what he did because he chose to." Giving him a sad smile, she shook her head. "There was nothing you could have done to stop him."

"I know that," Colin whispered, his heart feeling a thousand times lighter after hearing her say these words. "I know that it wasn't my fault, and yet, I cannot help but feel–"

"Guilty?"

Seeing tears spill over and run down her face, Colin pulled her into his arms, burying his face in her hair. "You feel it, too?"

She nodded against his shoulder as her fingers curled into the fabric of his jacket. "I've missed you, Colin."

Leaning back, Colin grasped her chin, tilting her head upward. Her brown eyes still shone with tears as she looked up at him. "I'm sorry I left," he whispered. "I didn't know what else to do."

"I understand," came her reply, soft and simple, and Colin knew that she meant it.

For a long time, they stood in each other's embrace, their eyes locked as they silently shared the pain they had endured over the past few years ever since they had lost their best friend…as well as each other.

10

THE FITTINGS OF AN OLD LIFE

Colin's first thought after learning of Jo's engagement was to leave London immediately.

Still, as much as he tried to convince himself that it was the right course of action, he could not bring himself to go. Whenever he was about ready to order his bags packed, her face would drift before his eyes, her own dark and full of sadness, and he knew he had to see her again.

While his heart ached for her grief, Colin could not deny that their short encounter the other day had changed him. He already felt lighter as though a mere look into her soulful eyes, those eyes that knew him so well, had somehow lessened his burden.

And so, he stayed, hoping to see her again, wondering if he should simply call on her. But what about her fiancé?

Attending a ball at the Dashwood townhouse, hoping that Jo would find her way there that night as well, Colin greeted Charles Dashwood, second son—by only a few minutes—of the late Lord Norwood. "Good evening, sir. I believe I've had the pleasure of meeting your brother, Lord Norwood, upon my stay in Italy."

Mr. Dashwood's eyes widened in surprise. "You have? I admit I haven't heard from Robert in quite a while. I hope he is well."

Colin nodded. "He is."

Considering they were twins, Colin was not surprised to see Robert's mirror image on his brother. Still, the resemblance ended there. While the younger brother looked like the image of a perfect English gentleman, impeccably dressed and his hair cut in the latest fashion, the older sibling had always reminded Colin of a pirate with loose-fitting clothes and his hair grown long and tied together in the back of his neck. While Mr. Dashwood appeared to be a dedicated historian, Robert had always travelled the world with no intention of ever settling down. As far as Colin knew he never stayed in England for long.

More than once, Colin had felt alone and abandoned during his years on the continent. Upon one such occasion, he had stumbled upon Robert Dashwood, Lord Norwood, in a drunken stupor and assisted him in locating his apartment. They had talked through the night until Robert had fallen asleep with his head on the table. After that, Colin had been glad to call him friend.

Although their ways had often taken them into different parts of the world, they had always stumbled upon one another here and there. Upon leaving Venice, Robert had bade Colin to give his brother his best and assure him that he was well…and lousy at writing letters.

Colin chuckled, "He had every intention of sending a letter to you but—"

"He couldn't find any ink or paper?" Mr. Dashwood asked, rolling in eyes in good humour. "Yes, I've heard that before."

"I assure you he does not mean to cause you unease."

"Robert never does." Mr. Dashwood paused, his gaze studying Colin's face. "But I suppose you know that."

"I'm aware, yes."

"Welcome then. I hope we'll have a chance to speak later," Mr. Dashwood said, his gaze honest, and Colin knew that as different as the two brothers were, they loved each other dearly. In truth, ever since meeting Robert and hearing from him about his twin Charles, Colin had felt reminded of his own relationship to Owen. Indeed, they had been different as well—perhaps not as much as night and day—but had always stood as one, there to offer aid whenever the other had had need of it.

It was a powerful bond and devastating once severed.

Colin hoped that Robert and Charles would never have to find out how that felt.

With slow steps, Colin stepped into the ballroom, his gaze sweeping over the attending guests as his heart beat with excitement as well as a hint of apprehension. Would she be here tonight? What would she look like not dressed in a simple dress, here and there torn from climbing trees and slipping through thickets, but in a gown accentuating those dark eyes of hers?

The answer was - magnificent.

Blinking, Colin swallowed when his gaze finally found her, standing in a small circle with her parents, her grandmother as well as…Kenwood and an older lady, presumably the man's mother. While the rest of her company chatted animatedly, Jo looked a bit forlorn, her gaze distant as though she was elsewhere. Still, the moment their eyes met across the room, that old spark returned to her dark eyes and the corners of her mouth curved upward into a delicate smile before she could stop herself.

Grandmamma Clarice noticed first, and before long her gaze followed her granddaughter's. When she spotted him, joy came to her face, and she instantly waved him over, whispering to her son and daughter-in-law, no doubt informing them of Colin's presence.

A bit of unease crept up Colin's spine, and yet, he could not deny that Grandmamma Clarice's joy warmed his heart. Always had he thought of her as his grandmother as well, and he had missed her dearly these past years.

"My dear boy, you're finally home," Grandmamma Clarice beamed as her pale eyes ran over him in frank perusal. "You've spent time in the south. Look at you. You're a far cry from all the pale-faced Englishmen I see day in and out." A soft chuckle left her lips before she reached up and enfolded him in her arms.

Leaning down so she could reach, Colin felt a bit awkward, but would not have wanted to miss this for the world. "I'm glad to be back," he told her when she stepped back, lowering herself back onto her heels. "It's been a long time."

"It's been too long," Grandmamma Clarice insisted. "Promise me you'll never disappear like that again."

Colin nodded, his gaze drifting to Jo, who stood in the back, her arm through Kenwood's, and glanced at him from under her lashes.

"Johanna, dear," Grandmamma Clarice called, her sharp eyes not missing anything, "this is a marvellous day, is it not? Our dear Colin is finally back." Holding out her hand, she pulled her granddaughter forward, all but pushing her into Colin's arms. "You haven't seen each other in…what?…four years. I'm certain you have a lot to talk about." And with that Grandmamma Clarice drew the others away, leaving him and Jo to look at each other like fools, not knowing where to begin.

Clearing his throat, Colin offered Jo his arm. "Shall we walk?" he asked, wondering what agenda Grandmamma Clarice had. After all, she had been the one to send for him. Had she known Jo had been on the verge of betrothal to another? Or had that been a more recent development?

"I'd like that," Jo whispered, and Colin got the distinct feeling that with all these bystanders around she did not feel like herself, nor dare act like it.

As they cut their way through the crowd, Colin spotted Mr. Dashwood standing with two young ladies as well as an elderly couple. Upon seeing them, he inclined his head, clearly interested in continuing their conversation and hearing further details about his brother's life.

Inhaling a deep breath, Colin decided that perhaps it was exactly what Jo needed. Something that would take the focus off them and allow them to converse with greater ease. And so, he steered her toward the other side of the ballroom. "Mr. Dashwood, it is a pleasure to see you again. May I introduce an old friend of mine, Miss Johanna Grey."

"It is a pleasure," Mr. Dashwood said, bowing to Jo, who managed a sweet smile, her hand tensing just a little on Colin's arm. He had to admit he rather liked it, for the moment selfishly—or foolishly! —ignoring that the woman he longed for was betrothed to another.

After Mr. Dashwood introduced those in his company as Lord and Lady Gadbury as well as their daughters Lady Isabella and Lady Adriana, he asked, "Has Robert said anything about returning to England?"

Colin shook his head. "I'm afraid not. When I left Venice, he was planning on travelling to Greece next."

"Greece!" Lady Isabella exclaimed, a touch of awe in her voice while her sister rolled her eyes, clearly bored. "What a wonderful country so rich in history and archaeological sites."

While Lady Adriana and her parents quickly shrank into the background, Mr. Dashwood and Lady Isabella seemed most interested in the sites Robert planned to visit. "I assume you're aware that history is a passion of mine," Mr. Dashwood said, glancing at the young lady by his side. "Ours, truth be told." Colin wondered if they might be more than mere acquaintances…or would be eventually.

Colin laughed, noticing the relaxed smile that had come to Jo's face. "Robert mentioned your interest."

Mr. Dashwood laughed, "We're quite unlike one another in that regard. My fascination with history and ancient artefacts has always bored Robert to tears."

Lady Isabella chuckled, glancing over her shoulder at her sister. "It's been the same with me and my sister. She steadfastly refuses to go to the British Museum with me. It is strange to think that one and the same place can be utterly fascinating for one and utterly boring for another." Shaking her head, Lady Isabella sighed before her gaze drifted to Mr. Dashwood.

Beside Colin, Jo chuckled, "Let me guess, the two of you met at the British Museum?" she asked, glancing from the young lady to Robert's twin.

Colin smiled when he saw Jo reawakening, shaking off the gloomy thoughts that had no doubt lingered on her mind. If only he knew what they were!

Mr. Dashwood nodded, sharing a knowing look with Lady Isabella. "Indeed, we did. I found it quite refreshing to meet a like-minded lady in the one place I feel most at home. I'm afraid I do not know how to converse about fashion and horse racing and…whatnot." Mr. Dashwood grinned a bit sheepishly as though he was used to apologising for his passion. "It is utterly favourable to spend one's time with someone who understands the fundamentals of one's character, is it not?"

"I whole-heartedly agree," Colin said, glancing down at Jo in the very moment she looked up at him. The second their eyes met, he knew beyond the shadow of a doubt that she felt the same, and the bond that had connected them since childhood pulled on his heart with renewed force.

She was indeed the one, and he could curse himself for allowing her to slip through his fingers. Why had he not returned sooner? He had been a fool to wait this long.

Ten minutes! That thought had been circling through his mind ever since he had first seen her after returning to England. He had lost his chance by a matter of ten minutes! Was fate truly this cruel?

After taking their leave from Mr. Dashwood and Lady Isabella, Colin steered Jo passed dancing couples and whispering matrons, trying his best to be inconspicuous and not catch Kenwood's attention as he guided the man's fiancée through a side door and out into a darkened corridor.

"Where are we going?" Jo asked, a touch of concern in her voice as she glanced at the deserted hallway. "We should return to the ballroom."

Pulling her onward, Colin shook his head. "I need to speak to you," he bit out, cursing himself for the harshness of his tone. Then he opened the door to the library and led her inside, shutting it behind them. "Why did you accept Kenwood's proposal?" he demanded without preamble, wishing that he had the patience to speak to her the way she deserved.

However, he did not.

He needed to know.

Now.

11

A WORD GIVEN

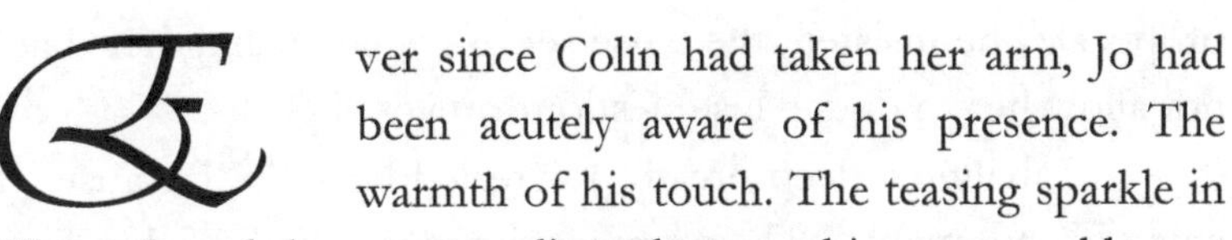

Ever since Colin had taken her arm, Jo had been acutely aware of his presence. The warmth of his touch. The teasing sparkle in his eyes. The soft curl that came to lips whenever his gaze would meet hers.

And again, she had felt that flutter in her stomach that only he had ever stirred within her.

Renewed guilt had welled up in her heart; not only for Owen's sake, but now for Brendan's as well. Was this her fate? To betray the man she was betrothed to?

Ever since Colin's return, Jo had done her utmost to ignore the deep longing that had suddenly returned to her heart. She had tried to tell herself that he was merely a friend, that she cared for Brendan, but it had been no use. Her heart had called her a liar.

And yet, she had given her word.

This time it had been her choice. Not her parents'. It had been she who had chosen to accept Brendan's proposal, promising him her heart, her loyalty, her future.

"Why did you accept Kenwood's proposal?" Colin all but snarled as he stood before her, his large frame blocking the door, forcing her to answer.

Jo swallowed, overwhelmed by the sudden confrontation. Only moments ago, she had begun to relax in his company, finally able to see past the guilt that had reclaimed her ever since his return. And now, here he was, asking the very question she feared more than any other.

Why indeed? For deep down, Johanna knew that it had not been love that had urged her on. No, if she was utterly honest with herself, she knew that it had not been.

Still, this was not the time and place to be utterly honest, and so Jo raised her chin and met Colin's burning gaze with a defiant one of her own. "How dare you snap at me like this? Have you no manners?"

A dark chuckle rose from his throat as he stalked toward her, the green in his eyes darkening with each step. "Why did you accept his proposal?" he insisted, the tense set of his jaw telling her that he would not allow her to dodge his question forever.

Inhaling a deep breath, Jo steeled herself. "Because…because I enjoy his company." The moment the words had left her lips, Jo knew it was a weak answer, and she wondered where it had come from. If she was to convince Colin that she did not care for him, she had have to do better.

After all, she had given her word.

Colin snorted, "That's a rather odd way of saying that you care for him." His eyes narrowed as he watched her. "Do you?"

Gritting her teeth, Jo swallowed, willing herself not to drop her gaze. "Of course, I do," she bit out, crossing her arms in front of her. "Why else would I have accepted him?"

"That's exactly what I want to know," Colin replied as he strode forward, his long legs carrying him to her until the tips of his shoes brushed the hem of her gown. "I do not believe that you care for him, not the way you care for–"

"Of course, I do!" Jo interrupted before Colin could say what she feared most in this world. "He's a wonderful man. He is kind and respectful. He makes me laugh." She sighed, disgusted with herself when she noticed tears standing in her eyes. "I haven't laughed in so long. He helped me. He..." Her voice shook as she spoke, and the words died on her lips.

With his lips pressed into a thin line, Colin had been watching her. However, when her voice broke, he exhaled a long breath and his features softened. "He was a friend to you," he whispered as his hand reached out yet again and tucked a stray curl behind her ear. "A good friend."

Jo shivered at his touch, her muscles tensing to keep her from sagging to the ground as her knees turned to water. "He was," she whispered, reminding herself of the man she had agreed to marry. The man who was not the one currently standing in front of her.

Colin swallowed as a shadow fell over his face. "Like Owen."

In that moment, Johanna's heart stopped, and she stared at Colin open-mouthed, her being overwhelmed by the myriad of emotions that washed over her as the dam broke.

"Owen was a friend, was he not?"

Jo's mouth felt dry. "Of course, he was."

"Only a friend?" Colin asked, his green eyes narrowed as he watched her. His shoulders betrayed the tension that rested in his body as he waited for her to reply.

Johanna swallowed, not knowing what to say. Owen had been her friend and her betrothed, and she had owed him more than friendship, had she not? Was she betraying his memory by stating out loud that she had never felt more than friendship for him? Was she betraying him even now by merely thinking it?

"Do you know," Colin began when she remained quiet, too lost in her thoughts, "if *he* ever felt more for *you* than friendship?"

Oddly enough, Johanna had never asked herself that question, and yet, her heart seemed to know its answer as though Owen had proclaimed it himself. “No. He did not.”

Colin almost sagged forward in relief, a deep smile claiming his features. “How do you know?” he asked as though he did not dare believe her.

Johanna sighed, realising for the first time that she had not been the only one in their betrothal who would have chosen differently. “Because he never looked at me the way–” Breaking off, she clamped a hand over her mouth, her eyes wide as she stared at Colin.

Holding her gaze, Colin slowly reached for her hand, pulling it from her mouth. “The way I did?” he whispered, his heart on his tongue. “The way I still do?”

Johanna’s teeth began to chatter, and goose bumps broke out all over her body as an icy chill raced through her. Fear lodged the breath in her throat, and she took a step backwards, knowing the danger she suddenly found herself in.

“Don’t run from me, Jo?” Colin pleaded, his warm hand tensing on her chilled arm.

“I have to go,” Johanna mumbled, trying to push past him. But Colin still held on, pulling her back, this time straight into his arms. Warmth engulfed her, and for a moment, Jo wanted nothing more but to close her eyes and lean her head against his shoulder.

This was Colin. He knew her better than anyone in this world. He saw what went on in her head even when she did not say a word. Heavens, he knew her better than she knew herself. And he dared to speak his mind. If only she could be as daring as he!

“No, I have to go,” she insisted, fighting not only against his hold on her but also her own desire to simply admit the truth and act on it. When he would not let go, she looked up at him with pleading eyes. “Please, let me go. I’m betrothed.”

The moment the last word left her lips, Colin tensed, and yet, his embrace was as gentle as ever. “But you don’t want him,” he whispered. “You want me.”

Jo could feel her heart hammering in her chest…with fear as well as temptation. "But…but he's good for me." Although she knew now that she had missed Colin with all her heart these past four years, he was a constant reminder of the loss they had suffered. And as long as she could not make her peace with the past, she could not bear to look at him in the years ahead.

Colin's jaw hardened, and she could see resignation fall over his face. "I came to London," he whispered, his voice raw, "to ask for your hand."

Jo closed her eyes, her head sinking forward until her forehead came to rest upon his chest.

"Of course, the choice is yours. If you do not want me, I will go."

Panic swept through Jo in that moment, and her head flew up, her eyes finding his.

"Do you want me to go?" he demanded, his arms tightening on her as though no matter what her answer would be, he would keep her by his side.

"I gave my word, Colin," Johanna whispered as tears streamed down her face. "I cannot break it. I could not live with myself if I did. It would always stand between us." She shook her head in resignation. "I cannot break it."

For a long moment, Colin looked at her as though time had stopped. Then one hand grasped her chin, and for a split second, his gaze dropped to her mouth. "But you want to," he said, his voice harsh and full of agony.

For a brief moment, Johanna closed her eyes before she met his gaze once more, her heart daring her to be honest…even if only this one time. "Yes."

Colin swallowed, and his gaze hardened with determination.

Johanna was not certain what she had expected. Passion. Fire. Heat. Perhaps. But the agonising tenderness with which Colin placed his lips on hers stole the breath from her lungs. The tips of his fingers brushed over her cheek, teasing the sensitive skin below her ear and down the column of her throat. His other arm held her tightly in his embrace, safe and loved, while his lips whispered of the joys of a shared future.

A dream that could never be.

Then Colin stepped back, and his arms released her. Instantly, an icy chill returned to Johanna's body, and a deep emptiness filled her heart. Tears streamed down her face as she watched the sorrow in his gaze deepen and grow.

"I wish you only happiness, Jo," Colin whispered, his voice choked with emotions. "You deserve to be happy whether you believe that or not." Then he stepped around her and left the library, closing the door behind him.

Jo knew she would never see him again.

12

HAPPINESS AWAITS

The following weeks were a blur to Johanna, and she was grateful that Brendan's mother took over planning her wedding as she herself would have been utterly overwhelmed by the myriad of decisions that needed to be made even under normal circumstances.

Colin had left town only days after they had last spoken, and Johanna had done her utmost to pretend that he had never even come to see her. Although her grandmother tried to broach the subject, Johanna's vehemence soon ended the discussion. After all, there was no use in crying over spilt milk. Was that not what people said?

With each day that passed, Johanna's heart grew more resilient, shutting out everything that threatened to offset the delicate tranquillity she had found by way of separating herself from that part of her that only served to cause her pain. She willed herself to smile and laugh and reminded herself to be happy and to remember how fortunate she ought to consider herself.

After a while, a part of Johanna started to believe that she truly was.

Before long the night of their engagement celebration arrived, and Johanna found herself standing beside her betrothed, welcoming family and friends to join in their joy. The smile on her face reminded her of the time her mother had pushed her to meet London's eligible bachelors—had only a few weeks passed since then? —but Johanna sternly ignored all thoughts that did not serve a purpose. Instead, she concentrated on their long line of well-wishers, graciously accepting their congratulations.

"Are you all right?" Brendan whispered to her, his brown eyes warm and caring as they swept over her. "You look a little pale."

"I'm fine," Johanna insisted, the corners of her mouth curving a fraction higher. "I'm fine."

Brendan squeezed her hand. "I apologise for my mother," he whispered after accepting Lord Stanton's well-wishes. "I know she can be quite trying. I hope her meddlesome nature has not robbed you of the joy of planning our wedding."

"Not at all," Johanna assured him as the muscles in her cheeks began to ache. "I'm fine."

Then the next well-wisher claimed Brendan's attention, which gave Johanna the chance to inhale another fortifying breath and at least for a brief moment relax her face, allowing the smile to fade.

"Congratulations, my dear. We wish you all the happiness in the world."

Blinking, Johanna lifted her gaze, realising that her mind had momentarily drifted off to some far-off place where life was simpler and did not hurt as much. As her eyes focused on the elderly couple before her, the breath caught in her throat, and for a moment, she was certain she would faint on the spot. "Thank you," she mumbled as though in trance, "Lord and Lady Sawford. You're too kind."

Owen's parents.

Right here, in front of her were Owen's parents.

Johanna's jaw began to quiver as her gaze swept over Lady Sawford's kind blue eyes, not as bright and joyous as she remembered them, but with a silent strength that spoke of a tragedy suffered...and survived. Her husband bore a similar look in his eyes, and the way his wife's hand rested on his arm, his hand not only covering hers, but holding on, spoke of a deep bond.

"It is truly good to see you again, child," Lady Sawford whispered, her other hand gently coming to rest on Johanna's arm. "Don't look sad. This is a happy occasion."

Johanna swallowed, willing herself not to succumb to tears, and yet, it seemed impossible when she saw a faint shine moisten Lady Sawford's eyes as well. "Thank you," she whispered, not trusting herself to say more.

Lady Sawford nodded, exchanging a look with her husband. "We wanted you to know how happy we are for you. You deserve a wonderful man at your side, and we trust that you've chosen well."

Staring at Owen's parents, Johanna followed them with her eyes until they disappeared in the crowd. More than anything, she wanted to run and hide, be alone with the emotions that had flared up in her chest upon seeing them, but her feet would not move.

"Are you all right?"

Blinking once again, Johanna saw Caroline and Penelope standing in front of her, their faces blurred as they stood behind a curtain of tears. "I'm fine," Johanna repeated for what seemed the thousandth time that night.

"No, you're not," Caroline insisted, her dark eyes sweeping over Johanna before she turned her attention to Brendan. "If you'd excuse us, my lord, I believe Miss Grey is feeling a bit faint."

All concern, Brendan immediately offered to escort her away from the crowded noise of their engagement celebration.

Johanna thought she would suffocate.

Fortunately, watchful Caroline interfered. "There's no need. Tend to your guests, my lord, and allow us to see to our friend."

Though reluctant, Brendan nodded, his warm brown eyes lingering on Johanna for a moment before he turned back to his guests, his posture now tense as he wished he could simply step away and see to the woman he would soon call his wife.

Johanna felt ill.

How they made their way to the library, Jo did not know. Only when the door closed behind them did she look up and find herself alone with two of her most trusted friends.

"What's going on?" Penelope enquired, her blue eyes misting over as she looked at Jo. "I've never seen anyone so sad at their engagement party."

Wiping tears from her eyes, Johanna cleared her throat. "I'm not sad. I'm merely…overcome. That's all." Was that true? Johanna wondered. In that moment, she could not tell how she felt and why.

"It's us, Jo," Caroline reminded her, her voice gentle, but insistent. "You can tell us the truth. Nothing you say will leave this room. We promise." She glanced at Penelope, who nodded her head vigorously.

Johanna swallowed, and then said the first thing that slipped into her mind. "Colin came to see me."

A frown drew down her friends' brows for a moment. Penelope recovered first. "Oh, you mean Colin Grenville, your friend from…" Her voice trailed off when Johanna closed her eyes at the mere mention of his name.

"What happened?" Caroline enquired. "What did he want? I thought you had not seen him since…"

Johanna nodded. "I hadn't. When I returned home from Miss Bell's, my grandmother told me that he had left England. I didn't know he would return. One day, he…was simply there."

"He came to see you?" Caroline asked, a touch of suspicion in her voice.

Picking up on it, Penelope could not hide a wide smile. "Oh, I knew it!" she exclaimed. "He came back when he heard you'd returned home, didn't he? He came to see you because…" Her voice hung in mid-air as she waited for Jo to finish the sentence.

Licking her dry lips, Jo nodded. "He came to ask for my hand."

"And you refused him?" Caroline asked as Penelope jumped up with excitement.

Unable to hold herself upright any longer, Johanna walked over to the group of armchairs settled in front of the large hearth and sank into one with a deep sigh. "I didn't need to because he never asked me."

"Why not?" Penelope demanded, a touch of displeasure in her voice as she and Caroline walked over to join Johanna.

"Because when he called on me," Johanna began, a touch of madness tickling her mind at the thought of the mess her life had become, "I had just moments earlier accepted Brendan's proposal."

Penelope's mouth formed a somewhat shocked "O" while Caroline's eyes narrowed. "Do you regret your decision?" she asked. "Would you have accepted Brendan if you had known Colin…I mean, Lord Ashfield…wished to marry you?"

Closing her eyes, Johanna shook her head. "I don't know."

"That's not true," Caroline objected as her hand settled on Jo's, squeezing it not with compassion but with challenge.

Looking at her friend, Johanna was at a loss.

"She's right," Penelope chimed in. "I know you've never said anything, but I've always thought that there had been something between you and Colin from the way you talked about him. Have you never admitted that to yourself?"

Staring at her friends, Johanna felt as though she was losing her mind. "How could I have?" she all but snapped, feeling close to breaking down. Still, the steady hand resting on hers kept her grounded and sane. And so, Johanna inhaled a deep breath and finally allowed all her barriers to come down as the whole story came pouring out of her. Her friends listened the way they always had with compassion and without judgement.

Johanna spoke of her childhood, of the guilt she had felt after Owen's death, of the guilt she had begun to feel even before his death, of…Colin, of the way he made her feel, of how he reminded her of their loss…and of Brendan. Kind, generous Brendan, who deserved better than her.

Still, he had chosen her…and she had given her word.

"I understand what you mean," Caroline replied, her shoulders slumped as she sighed. "It seems timing was not on your side. You cannot break your word now, can you?" Always so certain, Caroline now sounded in doubt herself, like Johanna torn between what *was* right and what *felt* right.

"Of course, she can!" Penelope interjected, her wide eyes suddenly narrowed. "Love trumps all. As hard as it might be for Brendan to hear the truth, in the end, he'll be grateful." She squeezed Johanna's hand. "You cannot marry him if your heart belongs to another. *That* would not be fair. After all, yours was not a match of convenience. He cares for you, does he not?"

Fresh tears came to Johanna's eyes. "He does," she sobbed. "Heaven help me, he truly does. How can I tell him the truth? He'll be devastated. He'll hate me."

"Yes, he will," Penelope agreed, her voice gentle and filled with a wisdom beyond her years. "He'll hate you, and he'll have a right to do so. But he'll hate you even more if you allow him to marry you and then years later he'll come to realise that he wasted his heart on a woman who cannot love him. Don't make each other miserable," Penelope pleaded. "It's not too late."

"I think she's right," Caroline whispered as Johanna continued to stare at Penelope. "The truth is never the wrong course of action. It might be painful, yes, but it is never wrong."

As all strength left her, Johanna slumped down into her chair, her mind drawn back to the moment she had said goodbye to Colin. He had asked her then if she thought Owen had loved her, and she had denied it with a vehemence that had surprised even her.

And yet, it had been the truth. Owen had never cared for her the way Colin had come to. He had been her friend, her best friend, but nothing more.

All of a sudden, Johanna could not help but wonder what would have happened if Owen had not died that day. If he had not died, then perhaps the moment would have come where they would have spoken truthfully to each other of how they had felt. Perhaps knowing they could not make each other happy—not in that way—they would have gone against their parents' wishes and chosen a different path.

Perhaps.

Johanna liked to believe that they would have. After all, they had been best friends.

A soft smile came to Penelope's face. "You've made the right decision."

"What?" Stumped, Jo looked at her. "How do you…?"

"It's written all over your face," Penelope whispered, a touch of a smirk on her own. "You forget I've known you for a good long while myself."

Hugging her friends, Jo realised that for the first time in over four years she no longer felt torn. Certainly, she could not help but feel awful for what she would put Brendan through, but deep down she now knew that it would be for the best. Perhaps sometime down the line when he found a woman who would give him her heart, he would come to see that. Johanna could only hope so.

With her decision made, Johanna returned to the festivities, dreading the moment Brendan's kind, brown eyes would fall on her. Still, she would have to bear it as there was no way for her to speak to Brendan tonight. Tomorrow, she would call on him and tell him honestly how she felt. She could only hope it would not shatter his world.

Brendan deserved better.

13

A WRONG STEP

The hour was late when their last guests finally took their leave.

Johanna's feet ached, but not as much as her heart did whenever Brendan smiled at her or whenever his hand took hers, gentle and protective. Guilt and shame grew in her heart, and a selfish part of her wanted nothing more than to share what she had finally realised that night and have it be over with.

But Brendan deserved better.

It was like a mantra that she kept whispering in her mind over and over, and it helped her to make it through the evening with her sanity intact—at least as far as that was possible. After the past four years, Johanna wondered if she would feel truly at peace ever again.

Tomorrow morning, she would take the first step towards that goal and see where it would lead her.

"Good night, Johanna," Brendan said, smiling at her as he assisted her into the carriage. "Good night, Lord and Lady Rawdon." His gaze drifted back to Johanna, so full of hope and joy that it sent jolts of pain through Johanna's heart. "I shall see you tomorrow."

A cool wind blew that night, and Johanna began to shiver, relieved to be able to drop her gaze. "Oh, no, I forgot my shawl."

"I shall fetch it for you," Brendan beamed.

"Never mind," Lady Rawdon said, waving his concern away, but he had already darted back up the stairs to his front door. "That man is quite taken with you."

Unable to meet her mother's eyes, Johanna looked out the window, her gaze following Brendan until he disappeared inside his townhouse. Moments later, he reappeared, his mother by his side as they shared a few words.

Pulling her own shawl tighter around her shoulders against the chilling wind, Lady Kenwood stopped only two steps from the door, unwilling to step out into cool night air. Still, her lips moved, and Johanna saw Brendan turn his head toward her as he hurried down the steps toward their carriage.

What happened next would forever be imprinted on Johanna's mind, just like the moment Owen had lost his footing and fallen off the tree.

Why Brendan tripped, Johanna could not say as the night's dim light only granted her the barest of glimpses of her betrothed. It might have been the small puddle that shimmered slightly on one of the steps. Or it might have been that his foot came down on the edge of the step, offsetting his balance. Whatever the reason, the result was the same.

One moment, Brendan was smiling, his body upright and full of life, and the next, he was tipping over, sailing down the steps in a deadly angle before his head met the pavement not far from where their carriage stood waiting.

Unable to believe her eyes, Johanna stared at him, barely aware of his mother's screams, before her gaze fell on her shawl as the wind tugged on it, freeing it from Brendan's grasp and carrying it away on a cool night's breeze.

14

A NATURAL CONSEQUENCE

Holten Park, Summer 1817
Three Years Later

Standing below her window, Johanna glanced up at the tall ash tree, its thick, sturdy branches leading all the way up to her chamber.

Ever since she had returned to Holten Park three years ago, Johanna had thought about cutting it down more than once as it seemed to have become a constant reminder of the past. And yet, she had not for a part of her felt it only reminded her of the two young men whose lives had been lost because…

…because of her?

After about a year of hiding out in the country and mourning the two men who should not have left this world so soon, those around Johanna had begun to urge her to return to town and continue her life. To attend balls and look for a husband.

The thought had scared Johanna nearly witless.

While her mother feared she might before long be on the shelf, Johanna had concluded—when that had happened she could not say—that she would never marry.

Her friends had been shocked to hear her say so. All of them had found true love by then and happiness in their respective marriages, and all longed to see Jo equally happy. Still, Johanna knew that it was not meant to be.

Had she not been betrothed twice, only to see those men die before her eyes? Did all of London not refer to her as cursed, whispering about the poor men who had found their deaths because they had entered into an engagement to her?

Although neither her mother nor grandmother had spoken to her of those things, gossip had a way of reaching those it hurt the most. At first, Johanna had retreated to her chamber, crying her eyes out as guilt had reclaimed her once more. Over time, acceptance had settled in, and oddly enough, after a while, she had found a certain measure of peace.

Still, her grandmother had been the most vehement to argue with her. "You cannot truly mean to remain here for the rest of your life? You're still young. Do you not wish to have children? To fall in love?"

Unbidden, an image of Colin had entered Johanna's mind at her grandmother's inconvenient reminder, and Johanna could not deny that the thought of him still affected her. It had been three years since they had last seen each other, and yet, the memory of him was still as fresh in her mind as though it had only been a day.

Still, Johanna did not dare reach out to him.

"None of this was your fault," her grandmother had pointed out countless times. "You did not cause their deaths."

"I know," Jo had replied, and she had meant it.

Although an echo of guilt remained—how could it not?—something her mother had once said had helped Johanna understand the truth. Years ago, upon one of their first breakfasts in town, Lady Rawdon had said, *Nothing is without consequence. And while Johanna acted wrongly, she is no more to blame for poor Owen's death than I am.*

Back then, Johanna had not been certain what precisely her mother had meant to say with that. But later, speaking to her grandmother had helped her realise that no one was indeed an island, that all lives were connected in some way and, thus, influenced one another. Deeds had consequences, nothing more.

Only too well did Johanna remember how Lady Kenwood had spoken to her son when he had hastened down the steps. Was Brendan's mother to blame because she had distracted him? Was Brendan to blame because he had not paid heed to where he had stepped?

As her eyes swept over the old tree, Johanna sighed. If Lady Kenwood had known she would distract her son, she would have sewn her lips shut. If Brendan had known he would fall, he would not have offered to retrieve her scarf.

If only…

People made mistakes, and as long as there was no bad intention, fault could not be assigned. Should not be assigned, for no one could predict the future. All anyone could ever do was live their life.

Of course, that had prompted Grandmamma Clarice to argue that Johanna ought to do more with her own, that she ought to write to Colin and ask him to return to England. She had even threatened to do it herself when Johanna had refused.

Still, Johanna had remained steadfast for a small part of her—a part that knew no reason, no logic, no sense—feared that the whispers might be true.

That she *was* cursed.

That these men had died because of her.

That Colin would be in danger if he were to return and ask for her hand.

And that Johanna knew she would never allow to happen.

Never.

15

ONE DAY IN PARIS

"It looks like you're packing," Colin observed as his gaze swept over the open armoire and packed bags set around Robert's apartment in Paris.

Grinning, Robert Dashwood, Viscount Norwood, nodded. "That's because I am," he replied, sitting back in his favourite armchair, his long hair tied in the back and draped on one shoulder, a glass of brandy in his hand.

Colin shook his head, unable not to return his friend's grin. Robert did indeed look like a pirate, especially with that wicked gleam in his eyes! He was a bit of an odd man, but a true friend…if the past three years were anything to judge him by. "Where are you headed?"

"Home."

Colin paused in the middle of seating himself across from his friend. "Home?" he all but croaked, then fell back into the seat. "You mean, to England?"

Chuckling, Robert nodded.

"Why?" Colin swallowed as any thought of England always brought back thoughts of Jo. Thoughts he ought to have banished long ago but could not seem to ban from his mind.

"Why don't you join me?" Robert suggested without answering Colin's question. "I'd love a travelling companion, and you're not half bad." Again, that wicked gleam came to his eyes as though he had just suggested something utterly scandalous.

By now, Colin knew that it was simply Robert's way of teasing those around him, and it was best to act as though one had not even noticed. "I told you I won't return to England," he forced out through gritted teeth. "Ever."

"So, you've said," Robert observed, his deep hazel eyes steady as they held Colin's as though daring him to say more.

Colin inhaled a deep breath, steeling himself against any and all arguments his friend could put forth. After all, the strongest one against ever returning to London was the thought of happening upon Jo…and her new husband.

Colin doubted he would survive such a meeting, and, therefore, it was far wiser to remain far away. As far away as possible. "So, why are you heading back?"

Setting down his glass, Robert reached inside his jacket and pulled out an envelope. "Apparently, my little brother is getting married."

A smile came to Colin's face as he remembered Charles Dashwood. "Let me guess, to a Lady Isabella?"

Robert shrugged. "The letter does not say. He merely threatens my hide if I don't return to England with the utmost haste."

Colin chuckled, "I wouldn't have thought your brother capable of such words."

"I may have rephrased them a little," Robert admitted with delight. "Still, the meaning remains the same no matter how polite one expresses oneself, wouldn't you agree?"

Colin nodded. Robert had a strange way of looking at the world, and yet, it suited him perfectly. A man who had decided to live by his own rules alone and not subject himself to the censure of others. He seemed utterly free of doubt and regret. Colin could not help but envy him.

"So?" Robert pressed, and his brows rose in challenge.

Colin inhaled a deep breath. "I've said on the topic all I wish to."

Robert nodded. "I know. I know. And yet, you haven't said much." Fixing Colin with a daring stare, he once more reached for his glass. "You've never even mentioned her name nor what exactly happened. All you've hinted at is that she refused you."

Colin felt his muscles tense at the memory of their encounter in the library. He had felt so certain that she would agree to marry him, and then all had fallen apart.

"You look miserable," Robert observed, shaking his head in utter disbelief. "It's been…what? Three years? Three years in which you've never even laid eyes on that woman. You cannot tell me that she still holds sway over you. That's ludicrous."

Colin shot to his feet. "If you wish to insult me, I might as well go."

"Don't get your feathers ruffled," Robert laughed, gesturing for Colin to return to his seat. "You know very well that I had no intention of insulting you. I'm your friend. I merely wanted to point out that it might be time to leave this lady behind you and start over." He sighed, "After all, there are worse fates than yours." Setting down his glass, he once more reached for the letter. "My brother writes of a young woman who has lost two of her fiancés in the past few years. London whispers of a curse." Grinning, he wriggled his eyebrows. "Now, that is what I'd call bad luck. Apparently, she's retreated to her family's estate, determined to remain unwed." Robert laughed, "I suppose that's a great relief to all of London's gentlemen."

Once again in the process of sitting down, Colin froze upon Robert's retelling of the woman's unfortunate tale as it immediately conjured an image of the day Owen fell to his death. "That woman," Colin croaked, feeling his skin crawl with a strange sense of foreboding, "did your brother mention her name?"

"I think so," Robert mumbled as he turned the parchment in his hands, his eyes flying over the words. "I think her name was…Black. No, not Black. Grey. Miss Johanna Grey." His gaze rose to meet Colin's. "Why? Do you know her?"

Shock shot through Colin, freezing his limbs and chilling his blood. Unable to keep himself upright, he plummeted into the armchair fortunately still situated behind him. His thoughts raced, and yet, they felt utterly slow, unable to process the words he had just heard.

"You cannot be serious!" Robert exclaimed, a snort spilling from his lips. "Miss Grey is the mysterious woman who refused you? To marry another? A man who—according to my brother—didn't make it to the wedding?"

"Thank you for summing that up," Colin forced out through gritted teeth as his mind began a quiet chant, *She's not married!*

Although it felt wrong to feel joy at the thought that yet another man had died, freeing Johanna from yet another betrothal, Colin could not help the warmth that suddenly spread through his body, chasing away the icy chill that the mention of her name had first brought upon him. "She's not married," he whispered, almost breathless.

"How does that change things?" Robert asked, brows knitted in confusion. "She refused you. She chose that other man. She's probably heart-broken over his loss."

Colin swallowed, tensing at the thought of what this had done to Johanna. "I can only hope the guilt did not overwhelm her." He cursed under his breath. "I should never have left England."

"The guilt?" Robert enquired, the frown on his face darkening. "Why would she feel guilty?" His eyes widened. "You don't think she had anything to do with her fiancé's d—"

"Of course not!" Colin snapped. "But she already felt at fault when Owen—" He shook his head. "It doesn't matter. You wouldn't understand."

"Let me guess," Robert said, a grin on his face, "you'll return to England with me after all?"

Colin nodded, his hands clenching on the armrest as he thought of seeing Johanna again after telling himself for three long years that he had to forget about her.

"Do you truly think she will accept you now?"

Colin shrugged. "I don't know. But I have to see her."

"What if she refuses you again?"

"Then at least I'll know how she truly feels."

"Sounds like a plan," Robert replied, a hint of concern tinging his voice. "I only hope she's worth all this misery you've been through in the past three years."

"Believe me, she is," Colin whispered. "You'll understand once you lose your heart to someone."

For a moment, Robert stared at him before he broke down laughing. "I think I'll have to take your word for it as I'm not the kind of man who *loses* his heart to anyone. Believe me, it's better this way. Far less complicated from the looks of it."

Colin smiled knowingly. "Do as you wish, but don't think you've got a choice in this. No one decides to fall in love."

Robert grinned back at him. "Well, then I'll simply decide *not* to fall in love. That should work, shouldn't it?" Rising to his feet, he gestured to his packed bag. "You'll better go and grab your things. I'll be leaving within the hour."

Chuckling at Robert's innocent idea of love, Colin returned to his own apartment and hastily stuffed a few things into a bag before heading back to meet his friend. As worldly as Robert was in every other way, he apparently knew nothing of love. Colin wished he could be there when Robert would finally lose his heart…and realise there was not a damn thing he could do about it!

Together, they made their way back to England. While Robert headed back to Bridgemoore to attend his brother's wedding, Colin lost no time in reaching Holten Park, his thoughts focused on Jo. Three years had passed since they had last seen each other. Three years since they had last spoken. How had she dealt with the newest tragedy to find her? How had she survived? And how had it changed her?

Colin felt his skin crawl at the thought of all her fire and vivaciousness buried beneath bitterness and pain. He could only hope she had found a way to remain herself.

He cursed under his breath. He truly ought to have been there for her. Both times, he had run. Both times, he had left her alone. If only she could forgive him for that.

As the carriage drew to a halt in front of the large manor house, Colin stepped out, his gaze sweeping over the familiar building of his childhood. Oddly enough, his head turned to the side as though he expected to see Jo and Owen come walking around the corner. Did she feel it too? He wondered, the strange connection between past and present that seemed to linger here? How did she live with it day in and out?

Taking a step toward the front door, Colin stopped when an old tug jerked on his heart. A smile came to his lips, and without another thought, Colin turned away from the door and rounded the house from the east. The sun shone warmly on his head, and images of his youth returned. Not the mournful ones of the past years, but those that he knew he would treasure for the rest of his life.

When his gaze fell on the tall ash tree below Johanna's window, Colin felt momentarily reminded of the day he and Owen had come here to free her from her mother's punishment. For a bare moment, the image of Owen lying dead at the base of the tree flickered before his eyes. Fortunately, it was quickly replaced by the sight of his friend laughing, his face eager and full of adventure. Indeed, this was the best way to remember Owen.

His life.

Not his death.

Always would they have the memories they had shared. Always would Colin remember the wonderful friend Owen had been as well as the adventures they had embarked upon together.

He owed him that.

Stepping up to the tree, Colin inhaled a deep breath. While he would never forget Owen, he could not allow the past to keep him from moving forward. And so, he placed a hand on one of the lower hanging branches and pulled himself up.

16

A WICKED CURSE

itting in her favourite armchair under the large window, Johanna welcomed the warmth of the morning sun on her face as she allowed her mind to get lost in another adventure. Her heart beat steadily, and yet, with a hint of excitement as she turned page after page, safe in the knowledge that nothing in this story could affect her own life.

Johanna had come to realise that it was by far more preferable to embark on adventures from the safety of her bedchamber than to venture out into the world. She had tried it before, and she could do well without the heartbreak it had caused her.

It was in that moment of utter peace that a shadow fell over her, blocking the warming sun and darkening her world.

"What?" Jo mumbled as her gaze lifted off the page and turned toward the window. Then her eyes widened in shock, and the book clattered to the floor as her heart slammed to a sudden halt.

For outside her window, perched on a thick branch, crouched the man who held her heart.

Colin.

A teasing grin stood on his face as he knocked on the window. "Is there any chance you'll let me in?"

Suddenly jerked from her paralysis, Jo shot to her feet, panic still widening her eyes. As fast as she could, she threw open the window, her hand reaching for his. "Come quick!" she ordered as her voice trembled with fear. "Before you fall!"

Not perturbed in the least, Colin grasped her hand, his own warm against her chilled flesh, and allowed her to pull him through the window. However, the moment his feet came to rest on the floor by her abandoned book, she slapped him hard across the cheek. "Are you insane?" she snapped, her jaw trembling as she flung curses at his head, berating him for risking his life. Her hands grabbed the front of his jacket, and despite his significantly larger frame, she shook him with surprising strength, her limbs fuelled by fear.

Watching her, Colin smiled as though her anger pleased him, as though she had just confessed that her heart was his and had always been. Could he truly read her that well? Did he know? Perhaps he did, after all, one did not fear for someone one did not love, did one?

After a while, all strength left Johanna, and she all but sagged against him, her forehead coming to rest against his chest as she breathed in and out slowly.

"I'm sorry I frightened you," Colin whispered into her hair as his arms pulled her deeper into his embrace. How long had it been since he had last held her?

Too long.

Johanna only too well remembered their shared moment in the library years ago, and she felt herself respond with the same longing as she had then.

"How are you?" he whispered, his voice tentative, and yet, urgent as though a part of him was eager to receive the answer that had brought him here, unable to wait, to take it slow and enjoy a moment of peace.

After all, why else had he come if not to renew his intentions? There was no other explanation, and Johanna knew she ought to crush his hopes—as well as her own! —before they rose too high.

A deep sigh left her lips before she lifted her head, her brown eyes wide as they met his. "I was fine until a moment ago."

Grinning, Colin held on tighter when she tried to pull away. "Are you saying you're not happy to see me?"

Her brows knitted together, and she gave him such a disgusted look that he almost laughed. "I'm not happy to see you climb in my window," she snapped, and for a second, she was tempted to slap him again. "What on earth possessed you to do so?"

Colin frowned. "Correct me if I'm wrong, but I've climbed in your window numerous times, have I not? You never seemed to mind before."

Her nose crinkled, and her lips pressed into a thin line as Colin regarded her with something akin to mock bewilderment. "What are you doing here?"

"Are you not happy to see me?"

"Will you answer the question?" she snapped before she shoved hard against his chest, freeing herself from his embrace.

Colin swallowed, and his gaze darkened, losing all humour. "I heard what happened."

Again, her brows knitted together. "You heard what?"

"I heard that your fiancé passed away."

"Oh." For a reason Johanna could not name, she had always told herself that he knew. Perhaps believing it had put her mind at ease as it no longer meant that upon learning the news, he would come rushing back to England…and she would have to refuse him a second time.

And yet, here he was.

Colin shrugged. "When you…refused me, I left England." He sought her gaze, and Johanna could not bring herself to look away no matter how much she wished she could. "I left, and I didn't look back."

"I understand," Johanna replied, willing her chin to remain up. "You were right to do so."

Colin frowned, a hint of anger coming to his emerald gaze. "No, I was not. I should have stayed to ensure that you were all right. But I simply left. Again."

Hearing the pain and regret in his voice, Johanna steeled herself. "It is not your duty—nor was it ever—to ensure that I'm fine. We're friends. Nothing more."

With each word she had spoken, Colin's gaze had hardened. "You do not truly believe that," he demanded, advancing on her. "After last we spoke, it was quite clear that it was only your previous engagement that stood between us." He inhaled a slow breath, and briefly his gaze dropped to her lips. "You made that very clear."

Overwhelmed by the myriad of emotions his lingering gaze elicited, Johanna took a step back. "I apologise if I gave you a wrong impression. I assure you I had no intention of—"

Shooting forward, Colin's hands seized her by the upper arms. "Do not lie to me!" he snarled, pain more than anger contorting his face. "We may not have seen each other in many years, but I still know you better than anyone." His brows rose in challenge. "I can see that you're lying. I can see that you're afraid and that you're trying to hide it. What I don't understand is why! Why would you push me away when in truth you want me as much as I want you?"

His open admission took Johanna's breath away, and she stared up at him, her limbs beginning to tremble as hope once more blossomed in her heart.

In her mind's eye, she could see a future with Colin, a life shared, full of laughter and joy and happiness. She could see evenings by the fire and picnics on warm summer days, their children running through the tall-stemmed grass as they themselves once had.

Johanna could see all that. More than that, Jo *wanted* all that.

And yet, when she closed her eyes she would forever see Owen and Brendan lying dead at her feet, London's whispers of a curse ringing in her ears.

A part of Johanna urged her not to listen. It was the same part that had on occasion encouraged her to write to Colin after all.

But fear was a strong opponent, especially when one did not fear for one's own life, but for the life of someone one loved.

"Perhaps I did want you," Johanna admitted, her gaze almost unblinking as she stared up at him. "Once." Shaking her head, she held his gaze as her heart broke into a thousand pieces. "But now everything is different. I've changed. I no longer want what I once did. I'm sorry if this hurts you, but I think it would be better if you simply left." Her voice almost broke on the last word, and Johanna felt her teeth press together painfully to keep from sobbing into Colin's shirt.

For a long moment, he watched her, his face intent and almost free of the anger she had seen there before. Then the hands on her arms relaxed as something dark momentarily sparked in his eyes. "All right," Colin relented as though her words had not touched him. "But before I go, may I kiss you goodbye?"

Jo froze as the memories of their first and only kiss returned as though it had happened only the day before and not three long years ago. Again, Jo felt her knees grow weak and her breath quicken. Her body itched to be held in his embrace, and she wanted nothing more but to feel his lips on hers yet again.

"No, you may not." Swallowing, Jo lifted her gaze, trying her best to appear steadfast and confident, knowing that if he were to kiss her, her resolve would no doubt wither and die. No, she needed him to leave.

Now.

"Why not?" Colin demanded, and the corners of his mouth curved upward as though he was pleased by her answer.

Johanna swallowed hard. "Because…"

Inhaling a deep breath, Colin stepped toward her, his green eyes fixed on her face. "Why are you lying to me?" he demanded, and

Jo belatedly realised that she had just failed his test. "I can see that you're afraid. Why will you not tell me what scares you so? What is so awful that you're willing to forgo all the happiness that would surely await us?" Frustrated, he glared at her. "If you truly want me to go, then you need to tell me the truth. For as long as you lie, know that I will remain right where I am." His brows rose in challenge. "Nothing but the truth can move me."

Stepping back, Johanna buried her face in her hands as her feet began to carry her around the room. Her limbs ached with utter frustration, and her strength began to wane. "Why do you have to be so stubborn?" she snapped, spinning to face him, welcoming the anger that suddenly surged through her body. "Why can you not simply believe me? Have I ever lied to you?"

Colin shook his head, his gaze as determined as her own as he stepped toward her. "You have not, which is why I don't understand what makes you think you can lie to me now. Tell me! What frightens you so?"

"Nothing!"

"That's not true!"

"How would you know?"

"Because I know you!" Colin snarled, anger darkening his cheeks. "Now, tell me!"

"No!"

"Aha!" he exclaimed in triumph. "So, you admit you *are* frightened!"

Jo stemmed her hands onto her hips. "I did no such thing! Don't put words in my mouth! I've told you that before."

"Then answer me!"

"No!"

"What are you afraid of?" Again, gripping her by the arms, Colin brought his face close to hers, his eyes almost desperate as he spoke. "Damn it, Jo! Tell me!"

At the sight of his pain, Johanna felt her own anger subside. Exhaustion washed over her, and she no longer had the strength to hold him at bay. Perhaps she ought to be honest with him. Perhaps he deserved to know why they could never be. Perhaps then he would understand…

…and leave.

Her shoulders slumped as she lifted her gaze to look at him. "I'm afraid of what might happen if I don't send you away," she whispered, willing him to understand that this decision did not stem from a lack of feeling on her part, but rather the opposite.

His brows knitted in confusion as he looked at her, searching her face as he clearly did not understand. "What might happen to me…," he mumbled, shaking his head. "What do you m–?" Then his gaze suddenly widened. "You cannot truly mean those ludicrous whispers about a curse, can you?"

Jo could not fault him for thinking her insane. She would have probably done the same had anyone else spoken to her the way she had just spoken to him. Of course, her rational mind had argued countless times against the existence of curses. Of course, it was nonsense! How could it not be?

And yet, a flicker of doubt remained.

"You are not responsible for what happened to Owen," Colin insisted, his green gaze steady, pleading with her to believe him, "or to Kenwood. Those were accidents. Tragic? Yes. But not your fault. You have to believe me."

Jo sighed, "I do believe you," she whispered, a soft smile coming to her lips as she looked up at him. Now that she had shared her innermost fears, she felt somehow lighter, unburdened. "I do believe you. I swear it. And yet, there is a part of me that…I cannot explain it." Shaking her head, she steeled herself for his next objection. "I cannot agree to marry you, knowing what happened to Owen and Brendan. There's a part of me that *knows* that I'd be risking your life if I did, and I cannot do that. Please understand."

Staring at her, Colin remained silent for a long moment, his green eyes sweeping over her face, trying to understand, searching for doubts, for a weakness he could use to convince her. Jo could see his thoughts as plain as day, and her heart rejoiced at the deep emotions that fuelled him. He wanted her. He truly wanted her. A part of her had hoped for this all her life.

"I love you," he finally whispered, incredulity filling his eyes, before he shook his head in disbelief. "I always thought that would be enough."

Jo nodded, savouring the moment, knowing it would be the last they would ever share. "I love you as well," she replied, a bit of a shy smile tugging on the corners of her mouth. "I have for so long that I hardly know who I am without you." She inhaled a slow breath, fortifying herself for what needed to be said. "But I'd rather live without you and know you're alive and well somewhere than to see you laid to rest before your time." Tears came to her eyes, and she took a step back as he reached to pull her into his arms.

"Jo, please!" The longing in his voice broke her heart.

"No," she replied hardening her voice, knowing that she needed to close the door on a shared future all the way, or he would always have hope, and it would keep him from living his life. "You can ask me as many times as you wish, the answer will always be no."

Defeated, Colin stood before her, utter sadness clinging to his features. "I cannot believe this is happening. I always thought…"

Johanna nodded. "As did I. I suppose we were both wrong." She swallowed as her hands started to tremble, and her body began to ache so acutely that she thought she surely must be ill. "Please leave," she whispered, fighting to hold back, to keep the tears inside.

Despite the reluctance she could still see in his eyes, Colin nodded. "Very well. If this is what you wish." Then he turned back to the window.

"No!" Johanna exclaimed, rushing forward. "Through the door. Please!"

A sad grin came to his face. "We're not betrothed, so I should be safe from the curse, don't you think?" A moment later, he perched back on the ash tree's thick branch, his lips whispering a silent goodbye, before he made his way down to the ground. Only once his feet had settled on the fresh grass did Johanna breathe a sigh of relief.

Then she stepped back, closed the window and sank to the floor, her knees buckling as tears spilled forth.

He was truly gone.

17

GRANDMAMMA CLARICE

ith all his hopes crushed beneath his feet, Colin sank down onto the grass, his back resting against the tall ash tree. A part of him still could not believe what had just happened, that she had truly refused him. And yet, his heart rejoiced at the memory of her confession. She did love him. She always had. And yet, there was no future for them. How could this be?

"You look defeated, my boy."

Blinking, Colin was surprised to see Grandmamma Clarice standing only a few paces away. Her pale eyes watched him as they always had, and he got the distinct feeling that she was displeased with him. "Grandmamma Clarice," he greeted her, pushing himself to his feet. "It is good to see you."

The old woman's eyes narrowed. "You broke your promise."

"I did?"

"You promised me you'd never disappear again," she chided as he approached, her watchful eyes missing nothing. "You disappointed me, and now you need to make amends."

"I'm sorry," Colin offered, truly regretting that he had hurt the only grandmother he had ever known. "Truly, I am. Please tell me what I can do. Anything you wish."

A sly smile came to Grandmamma Clarice's face. "Marry my granddaughter."

A chuckle escaped Colin's lips before he stilled, his gaze going wide when he came to realise that she was not jesting. "Marry Jo?"

Grandmamma Clarice nodded. "You love her, do you not?"

Somewhat taken aback, Colin inhaled a deep breath. "I do, yes, but…"

"There are no buts when it comes to love," the old woman whispered mysteriously, a somewhat wicked gleam in her eyes that made Colin wonder about the young woman Grandmamma Clarice had once been. "Well then?"

Colin shook his head to clear it. "I'd marry her in a heartbeat," he stated, feeling his heart beat with more strength than before as hope returned into every fibre of his body. If he truly had Grandmamma Clarice on his side, perhaps all was not lost. But what could they do when Jo was so vehement in her decision?

"Then do so," Grandmamma Clarice replied with a chuckle as though he was being a fool for not seeing something that was right before his eyes.

Colin groaned, running a hand through his hair. "She won't have me," he replied honestly. "I tried, but she asked me to leave."

The old woman's eyes widened. "And you complied?"

"I can't force her into marriage!" Colin exclaimed, wondering if Grandmamma Clarice's mind was not as sharp as it once had been.

Another chuckle left the old woman's lips. "Sometimes those in fear cannot see reason," she explained, her eyes drifting sideways for a bare second as though she was remembering something of her own past. "Sometimes they need a bit of a push." The left side of her mouth curled into a sly smile. "Sometimes even a shove."

Unable not to, Colin returned her smile before his gaze wandered back to the large ash tree, his eyes following the strong trunk and thick branches until they fell upon Johanna's window.

"I know that my granddaughter loves you," Grandmamma Clarice stated, and the conviction in her heart chased away the chill that had settled on Colin's limbs. "She always has."

"Did she tell you?"

"She didn't have to," the old woman replied as her gaze travelled upward as well, lingering for a moment on her granddaughter's window before returning to him. "I know that she is afraid, that she fears for you, and at least right now, she cannot overcome that fear. You'll have to do it for her."

Colin frowned. "What? How? What can I do to convince her?"

Grandmamma Clarice shook her head. "Do not try to convince her, for you would surely fail. My granddaughter is a stubborn one. No, in order to win her hand, you'll need to be…creative."

Colin's frown grew more pronounced. "Why do I have the feeling that what you're about to suggest will be far from…conventional?"

Grandmamma Clarice chuckled, "You know me too well, my boy."

18

WHOSE WEDDING DAY ?

Johanna spent the remainder of the day in her chamber, relieved that no one came to see her, not even Grandmamma Clarice. Everybody seemed to be otherwise occupied, and so Johanna allowed herself to mourn, to grieve for the hopes she had once had for a future that was now never to be.

Colin was gone, and he would never return.

The sky began to dim by the time Johanna brushed the last tears off her cheeks, straightened her dress and pushed herself to her feet. Even from her eastern window, she could see the far reaches of magnificent streaks of red and violet painting the sky, whispering of the night and a new day soon to come.

Surprised at how much time had passed, Johanna hastened for the door, knowing that supper would be served soon. As she hurried down the staircase, hoping her eyes were not as red-rimmed as she feared, she wondered why no one had come to check on her when she had failed to appear for the mid-day meal.

Truly, it was a day unlike any other.

Fortunately, supper passed without an enquiry after Johanna's current state. No one seemed to notice the absence of her smile or the lack of conversation on her end. While her father, of course, was as oblivious as always, neither her mother nor even her grandmother seemed to notice anything out of the ordinary. A part of Jo could not help but feel hurt.

Sleep proved elusive the next three nights as Jo tossed and turned, her mind again and again conjuring the few moments she had shared with Colin. Again, she saw the sadness in his eyes, the longing, the love. Gritting her teeth, she buried her face in her pillow lest she jump from her bed and write an ill-advised letter, begging him to return.

Not only would it no doubt have disastrous consequences, but Jo did not have any idea where to send it. Colin was truly gone no matter how much she might want him back.

"Good," she whispered into the dark. "This way at least my weakness will not put him at risk." And so, in the many moments that followed when Jo felt her longing for Colin grow to unbearable heights she would remind herself that she had sent him away for a reason: to protect his life.

On the fourth morning after Colin's departure, Jo willed herself to return to her normal daily activities. She rose early, washed and dressed and then after breakfast spent an hour sitting by her window, her thoughts at least momentarily distracted by the words on the pages before her. After all, it was by far more preferable to read about another's heartbreak than to experience one's own.

When she closed the book and set it aside, a knock sounded on the door and Grandmamma Clarice walked in. "How are you, my dear?" the old woman asked, and her pale eyes slid over Johanna in a way that suggested she knew more than she ought to. "You look not like yourself."

Sighing, Jo rose to her feet. "Colin came to see me a few days ago." Long ago, Jo had learnt that there was no use in lying to Grandmamma Clarice as the old woman seemed to be like a bloodhound when it came to lies, half-truths and the like.

"I see," her grandmother mumbled, and Jo wondered about the lack of surprise on the old woman's face. "What did he want?"

Jo swallowed hard, uncertain if she would be able to speak the words without breaking down. Balling her hands into fists, she held a tight rein on her body, willing it not to betray her. "He wanted to marry me." The words left her mouth in a rush, and she heaved a couple of deep breaths once they were out.

"And you refused him?"

Jo nodded.

"Even though you wanted to accept him?"

Meeting her grandmother's gentle eyes, Jo nodded again, no longer wondering how her grandmother knew the things she knew. "It is better this way. Safer."

Coming toward her, Grandmamma Clarice reached for Jo's hands. "Life is not always easy, my dear. It is not straightforward, and our path is often hidden from us. But if there is one truth I've learnt in my life, it's that when you come to be as old as I am, you do not regret the things you did." Sighing, she shook her head. "No, you regret the things you did *not* do, the things you let slip through your fingers because you were too afraid, too proud or too stubborn."

Feeling tears sting her eyes, Jo nodded. "I know, Grandmamma. I know."

"The day will come for regrets," her grandmother said, brushing a tear from Jo's face, "but that day is not today. Come with me, Child, and do not fear."

Confused about her grandmother's last words, Jo nevertheless followed her out of her chamber and down the stairs. Again, she rubbed at her eyes, wondering if the tears would ever stop or if she had to spend the rest of her life, hiding the misery of her heart from those around her.

Stepping into the drawing room, Jo was surprised to find not only her mother and father standing by the large hearth, but also Pastor Banning. The kind, old man with the receding hair line and thick bifocals smiled at her. "Good morning, dear. How good of you to join us."

Returning his greeting, Jo glanced from her parents to her grandmother. "Is something wrong? Are you ill?"

Grandmamma Clarice snorted in a rather unlady-like fashion. "Nonsense. I'll survive you all." Then she waved her hand at the pastor as well as her son and daughter-in-law. "Shall we get going? I'm not getting any younger."

"Certainly," Pastor Banning assured her as Johanna's parents took a few steps back and positioned themselves a little to the side, a strange look in their eyes. Never had Jo seen her mother look at her quite like this, a mixture of joy and impatience in her gaze. At the same time, her lips were sealed shut as though she feared words might jump from her mouth that were not meant to be heard.

"What is going on?" Jo demanded, feeling an icy chill crawl up her spine. "You all are acting quite unlike yourselves."

"Where's the groom?" Pastor Banning enquired.

"The groom?" Startled, Jo took a step back, her gaze darting back and forth between her parents, her grandmother as well as the pastor. "What are you talking about? Is someone getting married?"

"Yes. You."

At the sound of Colin's voice, Jo froze, and her eyes closed as though the developments of the past few moments were simply too many to handle. Still, she could not deny that her heart danced with joy at the mere sound of his voice.

Inhaling a deep breath, Jo turned toward the door, her hand holding on tightly to her grandmother's. The moment her gaze fell on Colin, her knees turned to water and she thought she would faint.

This could not be!

"What are you doing here?" she croaked, wondering that her mind was still capable of rational thought.

Grinning, Colin came toward her. "It's my wedding day," he told her, a wicked gleam in his eyes that was only tempered by the sense of apprehension that held him rather rigid. "I thought it prudent to be punctual."

"You're getting married? To whom?" Johanna asked as her mind echoed his earlier answer. *You!*

A heartbreakingly gentle smile came to his face as he reached for her hands, settling them in his own as though they belonged there. "I'm marrying you," he whispered, his emerald eyes watchful as he waited for her reaction.

"But…I already told you…I can't…I…" All rational thought seemed to have evaporated into thin air at the thought of the future he promised. "I can't."

Colin nodded. "Yes, you can. If the only reason you refused me is that you fear for me, then don't make that mistake. I promise nothing will happen to me." A teasing grin curled up his lips. "As you can see nothing *has* happened to me. Three days ago, I asked your father for your hand, received his approval and blessing and then hurried to London to procure a special license. You see there've been plenty of opportunities for me to…kick the bucket–"

"Colin!"

"–and yet, here I am, alive and well." As she tried to slap him for his jesting words, he only held on more tightly to her hands, pulling her closer. "Perhaps we're meant to be. Perhaps not. I cannot say I care. All I want is you, whether we were destined to be or not." He inhaled a deep breath, and all humour left his eyes. "We've already wasted so much time, let us not waste more. The thought of a life without you already feels like a wasted life. Please do not make it a reality."

Overwhelmed by his words, Jo felt her resolve weaken as her heart thudded wildly in her chest, reminding her of the young girl she had once been. Everything had seemed possible then, bright and promising. "But what if–?"

"There is no curse!" Colin insisted before she could finish. "What happens happens. Unless you pull the trigger or slip poison into someone's drink, you do not have the power to end another's life, do you hear me? Owen and...Brendan did not die because they were betrothed to you, but because...they took a wrong step, as tragic as it was. What happened was neither their fault nor yours. And I need you to believe that right now!"

Jo felt her jaw begin to quiver as though that part of her that still wanted to live life to the fullest was fighting its way to the surface. "I want to," she whispered, and her heart skipped a beat when she saw his answering smile. Joy stood in his eyes, bright and clear and for all to see, and Jo wondered if all this overwhelmed her so because joy had been all but absent these past few years. Was she truly to continue like this? Or did she dare reach for something more?

"I can see that you want to," Colin teased, his hands tensing on hers as he waited.

"Of course, I want to," Jo snapped. "That was never the question. It's only—"

"No!" Colin cut her off. "If you love me, then say yes, and to hell with everything else."

Laughing, Jo felt tears run down her cheeks for the thousandth time in the past few days, and yet, these tears felt different. Her heart thudded with excitement, and her whole body hummed with expectation. Oh, how she wanted this!

"Yes."

Colin's eyes went wide. "Yes?"

Grinning, Jo nodded. "Yes."

In the next moment, he pulled her into his arms and swung her in a wide circle that had Grandmamma Clarice jumping back lest she be knocked to the floor. Still, a deep smile stood on her face, and Johanna knew how truly happy her grandmother was for her. Deep down, Jo had no doubt who she had to thank for this. Somehow or other, Grandmamma Clarice had brought them all here together, forcing Jo to face her fear and dare to be happy again.

"Then let's get started."

Frowning at her betrothed, Jo teased, "Why the rush? Are you afraid I'll change my mind?"

Colin's brows quirked upward. "Can you blame me?"

A moment later, they all stood in their assigned places, their eyes aglow and smiles lingering on all their faces. Pastor Banning began his usual litany, and although Jo could not believe that this was indeed her wedding day, all her attention was focused on the man beside her.

With their eyes locked, they breathed as one, their hearts falling into a matching rhythm and their hands holding on to the other, a promise to share life's trials from here on out.

For one dark moment, Jo wondered if perhaps something might happen after all to prevent their wedding from taking place, and in truth, she would not have been surprised if the earth had opened up to swallow Colin whole. But nothing happened. The world did not end. The house did not collapse on top of them. And neither did Colin trip and break his neck.

He still stood smiling before her when the words that bound them together flew from Pastor Banning's mouth. In a moment, it was done. They were husband and wife, and Colin pulled her into his arms for a thorough kiss.

Well wishes flew from her family's lips, and Jo turned to hug her grandmother. "Thank you, Grandmamma. Thank you so much."

Grinning, the old woman sighed, a sly smile on her lips, none-theless. "I only did what I thought right. No more, no less."

"You knew better," Johanna whispered. "I should have known that."

Grandmamma Clarice shrugged, brushing a gentle hand over Jo's cheek. "Well, I won't say I haven't been saying that all alone. But don't worry, my dear, it's the curse of youth. The very young do not always see what is right in front of them. You'll see when you're an old woman yourself." She grinned at Colin as he came to stand beside Johanna, his left hand settling on the small of her back. "At least, now, you'll grow old together."

Looking at her husband, Jo drew in a deep breath. "Do you promise?"

"I promise," he whispered and pulled her into his arms, safe and loved.

For a long time to come.

EPILOGUE

A few weeks later

 warm breeze drifted in through the large double doors of Holten Park as guests moved between the terrace and the drawing room. A large table laden with food and drink sat in one corner, offering refreshments, while a small orchestra played in the other, its music drifting out into the gardens where children ran wild.

Just as Jo and Colin once had.

After their rather impromptu wedding, Johanna's mother had insisted on a large party to celebrate her daughter's marriage. "It's about time happiness returned to this family," she had said in her usual, somewhat cold manner. "I can't think of a better reason to celebrate." And yet, Jo did not fail to notice the small smile that played on her mother's lips whenever her gaze would linger on her daughter and new son-in-law.

Even Colin's father was in attendance.

To everyone's surprise, the news of his son's marriage had shaken him from his stupor. Locked in his grief, he had wasted years mourning the loss of his wife and forgotten the son he still had. However, once he had seen Colin with Johanna, something had changed. Perhaps he had felt reminded of himself, of how he had married the woman had loved. And it had helped him break free of the dark that had settled on his mind, finally allowing in the sun's warm rays.

"You look so very happy," Adelaide said when she walked up to stand by Jo's side, overlooking the gardens. "I've longed to see you thus."

Smiling, Jo turned to her friend. "I am. I never thought I would be, but I truly am. I cannot believe that I almost turned my back on this." Sighing, she shook her head. "It's a dream come true."

"I know how you feel," Addy beamed, her brilliantly blue eyes drifting to her own husband.

Jo nodded as her gaze swept over her friends from school. They had all come to share this wonderful day with her, bringing their husbands and children, to ensure that they would never lose touch and always share in each other's lives.

"Who are they?" Addy asked, nodding toward Lord and Lady Sawford as they made their way down the small slope and into the garden where Colin stood speaking to Caroline's husband.

Jo inhaled a steadying breath. "Those are Owen's parents," she whispered, remembering what her grandmother had told her. She had been torn about whether or not to invite them, not wanting anything to dampen the joy of that day. Still, it had felt wrong not to, and so Jo had sent them an invitation, expecting them to decline once they read the groom's name.

And yet, here they were.

Jo could only hope that they would not attack Colin for the part they believed he had played in Owen's death.

"You look tense," Addy commented, her brows slightly knitted. "Is something wrong?"

"I hope not," Jo whispered as she watched her husband turn to address Lord and Lady Sawford. Colin's face was tense, and even from a distance, Jo could see the sorrow that stood in his green eyes. Could it truly be that Owen's parents did not realise how much the loss of their son had been haunting Colin?

However, to Jo's utter surprise and relief, it was not a confrontation that she witnessed.

Not unlike the night she had spoken to Jo at her engagement celebration to Brendan, Lady Sawford approached Colin with a gentle smile on her face as well as regret shining in her eyes. She spoke quietly, and judging from the look on Colin's face, her words were neither attack nor insult, but rather an apology.

Moments passed, and then Lady Sawford embraced him as she had so many times before when he had been young. Drawing in a fortifying breath, Colin hugged her back, closing his eyes as he once more leaned into the woman who had raised him after his own mother had passed away.

Tears came to Jo's eyes, and the moment Colin once again opened his own, their gazes met, and she knew how much the loss of his foster parents had pained him.

But no more.

Certainly, the past was not unimportant, not to be ignored or forgotten, but it was still only the past. No more and no less.

And the future shone bright and friendly, beckoning them onward.

THE END

This novella is the prequel to the Forbidden Love Novella Series. If you enjoyed it, read on about how Robert Dashwood aka "Notorious Norwood" returns to England to attend his brother's wedding...only to fall head over heels for his brother's bride.

Discover how twin brothers Robert and Charles find true love when they least expect it in *The Wrong Brother* and *A Brilliant Rose.*

Beyond those two, many more love stories await.

ABOUT BREE

USA Today bestselling author, Bree Wolf has always been a language enthusiast (though not a grammarian!) and is rarely found without a book in her hand or her fingers glued to a keyboard. Trying to find her way, she has taught English as a second language, traveled abroad and worked at a translation agency as well as a law firm in Ireland. She also spent loooong years obtaining a BA in English and Education and an MA in Specialized Translation while wishing she could simply be a writer. Although there is nothing simple about being a writer, her dreams have finally come true.

"A big thanks to my fairy godmother!"

Currently, Bree has found her new home in the historical romance genre, writing Regency novels and novellas. Enjoying the mix of fact and fiction, she occasionally feels like a puppet master (or mistress? Although that sounds weird!), forcing her characters into ever-new situations that will put their strength, their beliefs, their love to the test, hoping that in the end they will triumph and get the happily-ever-after we are all looking for.

If you're an avid reader, sign up for Bree's newsletter at www.breewolf.com as she has the tendency to simply give books away. Find out about freebies, giveaways as well as occasional advance reader copies and read before the book is even on the shelves!

Thanks you very much for reading!

Bree

LADIES OF MISS BELLE'S FINISHING SCHOOL

A FORBIDDEN LOVE NOVELLA SERIES

For more information, visit
www.breewolf.com

LOVE'S SECOND CHANCE SERIES

For more information, visit

www.breewolf.com

CPSIA information can be obtained
at www.ICGtesting.com
Printed in the USA
BVHW070039160223
658635BV00001B/34